In *First, We Kill All the Lawyers,* vampire lawyer Donovan Trait survived repeated attacks by a serial killer. Now, after violating a marital agreement with the Vampire Coalition and several ancient Vampire Laws, Donovan and his newly-turned vampire bride are on the run.

In exchange for permitting a pure-blood vampire to marry a turned human, the Traits had agreed to allow vampire scientists to monitor the conception and birth of their children. But when Judge Shirley Magnusen Trait turns up accidentally pregnant on her wedding day, the fury of the Coalition is unleashed.

The tribunal recommends unacceptable punitive action and the Traits are forced to flee to a mysterious island of vampire nuns. The Traits are, by profession, seekers of the truth. But this time the truth may not set them free. In fact, it could start a revolution. Will the Traits escape the clutches of the Coalition and keep their babies safe? Or will their family be . . . eliminated?

This book is a work of fiction. Names, characters, places, and incidents either are products of the author's imagination or are used fictitiously. Any resemblance to actual events or locales or persons, living or dead, is entirely coincidental.

Ye Gods! The Law is an Ass!
Copyright © 2021 Seelie Kay
ISBN: 978-1-4874-3358-1
Cover art by Martine Jardin

Published by eXtasy Books Inc

Look for us online at:
www.eXtasybooks.com

Ye Gods! The Law is an Ass! Donovan Trait 2

By

Seelie Kay

DEDICATION

To seekers of the truth. May it set you free.

CHAPTER ONE: THE GROOM

Donovan Trait pivoted and scowled.

"You have the audacity to claim you bear no liability for your actions? You skimped on the smoke alarms and sprinklers and failed to install the required number of fire extinguishers in the apartment building formerly at Three Zero Two West Michigan Avenue. When a fire erupted in the middle of the night as a result of faulty wiring, my clients—eight entire families—were left homeless. Fourteen people were hospitalized. How can you possibly deny fault?"

"Objection, Your Honor. Counsel is badgering the witness!" The defense attorney stood and planted his hands on his hips.

Judge Hillary Lord's bright red lips curved up into a cruel smile. "Actually, I have been admiring Counselor Trait's restraint. Motion denied." She narrowed her eyes and gazed at the witness. "Please answer the question, Mr. Livingston."

The witness glared at Donovan. "Because I didn't know that the smoke alarms and sprinklers *were* faulty." The man's voice grew strident. "I was told everything was up to code. That the building passed all inspections. I have the reports. There is no indication anywhere that the building was not in compliance. I can't fix what I don't know." The middle-aged owner sat back in the witness chair and a self-satisfied smile crossed his face.

Donovan studied the man. He looked every inch a pretentious, successful businessman. Artfully arranged hair. A freshly shaved face. A tailored suit of fine quality. Shoes

1

bearing the shine of expensive leather. Even his argyle socks screamed money. And his hands. It was clear that this man was a stranger to manual labor. The buff of his most recent manicure was evidence of that. Livingston's only tell was the almost imperceptible twitch in his right eye.

Not that Donovan needed the twitch to discern that the man was lying. Donovan Trait, one of Chicago's hottest lawyers—according to Chi Town Magazine—was a vampire. Vampires could read humans like a book. The slight rounding of the pupils, the increased heartbeat, the stiffening of the joints. All were indications of a lie. The best actors in the world could not escape the laser focus of a vampire. After all, vampires were closer to humans than any other species.

The only real difference occurred in the genetic code. Through a twist of cruel fate—for humans—a vampire's senses were greatly enhanced and enabled them to detect even the slightest physiological changes in humans. Of course, that was not the only genetic anomaly. Vampires also had fangs—those pesky lateral incisors that emerged in times of anger or overwhelming sexual arousal—and an unfortunate lust for human blood. Thankfully, centuries of evolution had provided the Vampire Nation with the gift of control. They no longer needed to drain the blood of humans to survive. Vampire scientists had developed a pill that quenched that thirst and replaced the nutrients a human had formerly provided.

Vampires were still in the closet to humans, of course, primarily because humans had displayed an unfortunate lack of tolerance for anything that deviated from the norm. The list of horrifying acts perpetuated by humans onto anyone deemed different was long and growing. New controversies surrounding the cross-gendered were the most recent atrocity, but history had proven that what humans feared, they destroyed. The Inquisition, the Salem Witch Trials, and the internment and concentration camps during WWII were all evidence of the resilience of human hate. That meant the introduction of what was considered paranormal—vampires, Weres, fairies, and such—could very well result in persecution and death. So, while vampires existed in the human world, they were loath to expose their origins. The risk was just too great.

Donovan stalked to the plaintiff's table and picked up a single sheet of paper. He pretended to read it, hiding his annoyance at the witness. Finally, he emitted a dramatic sigh. He turned and strode back to the witness stand. "Mr. Livingston, have you ever seen this?" He handed the paper to the witness and another to the judge.

Livingston pulled out a pair of designer reading glasses and scanned the page. He paled and his lower lip trembled, but he responded, "This appears to be a copy of a check, written on the company account. But I don't know what it's for. I've never seen it before."

Donovan cocked an eyebrow to convey his disbelief. "Truly, Mr. Livingston? The check is for one hundred thousand dollars. How, as CEO of Livingston Construction, could you possibly be unaware of such a large amount? Surely, you aren't in the habit of gifting random people?"

Livingston shook his head. A slight sheen of sweat emerged on his forehead. "I have no earthly idea what this check is for."

Donovan chuckled. "Mr. Livingston, the check is written to Ronald Santuro. Do you know who that is?"

"I do not."

"Would it surprise you to learn that he is a clerk in the office of the Cook County Building and Inspections Department?"

Livingston shifted uncomfortably in the witness chair. "Of course, it would. I just said I didn't know him." He peered down his nose at Donovan, his glasses now balanced on the very tip of that extremity.

Donovan nodded at the paper Livingston held. "Whose signature is on the check, sir?"

Livingston flushed. "Well, mine. But this is one of those stamp thingies my secretary uses. She signs all of the company checks. That's her job."

Donovan grinned — his best *gotcha* smile. "Your secretary is Barbara Brewer, is it not?"

"Yes. Has been for about fifteen years."

"Fifteen years? So, you knew her before her marriage to Jonathan Brewer?"

"Well, yes. I attended her wedding. Why does that matter?"

"Because Ronald Santuro is her brother. Her maiden name was Santuro."

Livingston shrugged. "I did not remember that." He again peered down his nose at Donovan. "Are you suggesting my secretary has been embezzling funds?" His face screwed up in disdain. "No, that can't be true."

Donovan laughed. He turned to the jury and winked. "Actually, your secretary is willing to testify that this check was prepared upon your instruction, signed upon your instruction, and delivered upon your instruction. She will also testify that she contacted her brother upon your instruction and arranged a meeting, at which you offered her brother one hundred thousand dollars to *expedite* the paperwork for several building projects, including the very apartment building at issue in this lawsuit."

The jury and those sitting in the gallery gasped. Donovan planted his feet directly in front of Livingston and gazed at him. He cocked his head. "Tell me, Mr. Livingston, did you bribe Ronald Santuro to overlook your failure to comply with the building codes of Cook County?" Donovan held up his hand. "Before you answer, I should inform you that Mr. Santuro has been arrested for accepting bribes in his capacity as a public servant." Donovan checked his watch. "Exactly fifty-four minutes ago. So, let me ask again, Mr. Livingston. Did you pay Ronald Santuro one hundred thousand dollars to overlook your failure to comply with the building codes during the construction of the apartment building formerly located at Two Zero Three Two West Michigan Avenue?"

Livingston bowed his head, slunk into his chair, then mumbled something.

Judge Lord frowned. "I'm sorry, Mr. Livingston. I didn't get that. Nor did the jury. Please restate your answer. A little more clearly this time."

Livingston hesitated. Then he slowly raised his head. His expression was one of fury. He glared at Donovan and spat, "I refuse to answer on the grounds that it might incriminate me."

Donovan grinned. "Thank you, Mr. Livingston. Your Honor, I have no further need of this witness. I move that that this notarized copy of a check made payable to Ron Santuro be entered into evidence as Plaintiff's Exhibit Twenty-Three." He paused, then smiled. "The plaintiff rests."

The judge nodded. "We'll resume the proceedings in one hour." She prepared to slam down her gavel on its sound block, but paused and pointed to defense counsel. "I hope defense counsel has the good sense to pursue a settlement *before* we return."

Donovan entered the chambers of Judge Shirley Magnusen. "Darling, I've missed you." He bent over and planted a kiss on her lush lips.

Shirley laughed. She tossed her wavy blonde hair over a shoulder and her deep blue eyes gazed at Donovan. Her mouth curled up into a playful smile. "It's only been four hours since you saw me last. Four hours since you sent me off to work with a glow and an overstimulated heart. And that was after a long night filled with sensual delights. I thought you'd stay away for at least a day so I could recuperate."

Donovan smiled. "Livingston's lawyer begged me to settle over lunch. I got him to cough up a million for each displaced person plus medical fees and resettlement costs. Damn fool even threw in attorney's fees, which I will distribute to my clients. Case closed. So, I have the rest of the day off." He knelt next to Shirley and stroked her leg, running a finger under her skirt. He cooed, "I thought we could play *house*."

Shirley blushed and placed her hand over Donovan's, stopping its ascent. She sighed. "Unfortunately, I have a full docket this afternoon. With Judge Heffernon on maternity leave, we are all picking up the slack. I have no time."

Donovan frowned. "How unfortunate. Perhaps you should have taken the day off before your wedding."

Shirley rolled her eyes. "With your mother's help, everything is set. Flowers, food, the minister. The only problem will be the press and the paparazzi. I know the wedding of one of Chicago's Most Eligible Bachelors and the winner of the Hottest Lawyer title five years running is big news, but the media is already camped out at the church. Reverend Billings has repeatedly called to complain. He claims they have been very disruptive." Her hand swept his body. "Those reporters can't resist you. Over three hundred years old and you're still hot. Those piercing blue eyes, thick black hair, a body sculpted by the Gods, and an appendage for pleasure that ensures I will never again bed a human . . ."

Donovan grinned. "You think I'm hot, almost-wife? Why, that pleases me deeply. And what about you? You give every bombshell in history a run for their money." He again ran a finger along Shirley's upper thigh. "Jean Harlow, Veronica Lake, Diana Dors. You put their bodies to shame. All curves, all of the time." Gently, Donovan raised her skirt and spread her legs.

"Donovan, I don't think . . ."

"Oh hush, almost-wife. I just want a taste. Something to take with me while I spend my afternoon lollygagging, waiting for you to come home." He pulled her lacy black panties to the side and inserted a finger into her pussy. "Already wet, yet you have no time for a sensual encounter?" Donovan clucked his tongue. "You would put the law ahead of sex? Maybe I should reconsider my marriage proposal." He again ducked between her legs and swiped her lips with his tongue. His fingers played with her clit, then dove inside her. One finger, then two, then three.

Shirley moaned and began to buck against his mouth. Then she grabbed Donovan's head and yanked him closer to her mound. She squirmed and emitted sounds of ecstasy as her almost-husband drove her to the brink.

Donovan grabbed Shirley's hips and drew her clit into his mouth. He sucked on the tiny button until it became hard and stood at attention. Then Donovan reached around Shirley's hips and sought her nether hole. He pushed his finger inside.

Shirley squealed and shuddered. An expression of exquisite pleasure crossed her face. She cast an adoring gaze at her almost-husband. Then she simpered and sank into her chair, spent.

Donovan pulled his head from her center and ran his tongue across his lips, licking up her juices. Deftly, he reached into his coat pocket and removed a handkerchief. "I am tempted to leave all this evidence of your orgasm on my face, but I am afraid your secretary would throw a fit because I distracted you." He wiped his face, then grinned. "Admit it, almost-wife. You needed a break."

Shirley giggled. "I suppose I did. How wonderful that I have someone to remind me when these little interludes are necessary." She straightened her skirt and repositioned herself in her chair. Shirley's expression turned stern. "Now what about Reverend Billings? With your afternoon off, I need you to contact him and calm him down. I don't want a no-show minister at my wedding."

Donovan sat on a leather couch facing Shirley's desk and continued to wipe her juices from his face. When he finished, he offered it to her.

Shirley shook her head. "I'm about to kick you out of here so I can get ready for my afternoon on the bench. I just hope I don't lapse into any post-coital malaise." She pointed at Donovan. "Now, about Reverend Billings . . ."

Donovan chuckled. "It's not like the old bastard can't handle it. In the centuries since he was ordained, he has married world leaders as well as movie stars, and some very wealthy businessmen. He is used to the hoopla. He won't admit it, but he loves the attention."

A puzzled expression crossed Shirley's face. "Centuries? Is he a vampire, then? One of us?"

Donovan smirked. "He's a Were. A Wereserpent. Kind of ironic, considering Satan appeared as a serpent in the Garden of Eden and was responsible for the human race's loss of innocence. Now, a serpent spends his days trying to save humans from themselves. There's a disconnect somewhere."

Shirley's eyes narrowed. "Funny, I thought vampires weren't religious. Yet you know the Bible?"

"I'm afraid God struck the first blow when he forbade the drinking of human blood. We are clearly one of God's children. No one really knows our true origins. Some believe we bear a witch's curse, others that our blood was tainted by a bat, and still others believe we are, actually, defective children of God — that when He played with the human race to introduce disabilities and mental defects, his genetic engineering was off and he created vampires and Weres."

"And what do you believe, darling?"

Donovan puffed out his chest. "All myth, of course. We may have what humans consider genetic defects — our fangs, our sensitivity to the sun, our allergy to silver, and of course, our lust for blood — but those have to be weighed against our assets. Our superior intelligence, our enhanced senses, and our long lives. We clearly have a leg up on humans, and unlike that species, we have adapted and adjusted to changing times. Our scientists have created successful solutions to our sensitivity to the sun and our blood lust. And a little social engineering refocused the use of our fangs. They are weapons when in danger, but also tools for sexual pleasure. The only time our fangs emerge is when we are threatened or aroused." Donovan waggled his eyebrows. "And I haven't heard any complaints from my luscious wife-to-be."

Shirley grinned. "You know, I am a bit of an experiment. I have experienced thirty-two years of life as a human, and after my turning is complete, I will live out the rest of my life as a vampire. I am one of the few who will truly know the advantages and disadvantages." She peered through her thick brown eyelashes at Donovan. "What if I made the wrong choice?"

Donovan's eyes widened. "Surely you are not regretting your turning? It can be stopped, but it can't be reversed. You have already completed four treatments." Panic filled him. The Vampire Coalition had mandated Shirley's turning as a condition of their joining. Shirley had knowingly and willingly consented to a forced turning — the substitution of her human blood with a synthetic that mimicked vampire fluids and contained the stem cells and other genetic material of a vampire. "Ye Gods, please tell me you haven't changed your mind. I don't think I could survive without you. I . . . I . . . I . . ." Donovan buried his head in his hands. "Please, Shirley. Don't . . ."

Shirley giggled. She stood, pulled Donovan into her arms, and laid her head onto his chest. "Darling, you just made me come in the middle of the afternoon. No way am I giving that up. Besides, you know you're the only one for me. I am in, lock, stock, and . . . er . . . fangs. I love you. Only you."

Donovan cupped her chin and drew her lips to his. His desire for her was overwhelming. He had finally found that missing piece. The one thing that had eluded him throughout the centuries. Donovan didn't know what the future held, but he did know he wanted Shirley at his side.

His fangs lightly brushed her lips as his arousal became clear. Shirley angled her neck, and he nipped down to her lush breasts. With due care, of course. It wouldn't suit for his lovely fiancée to bear fang marks on the bench. Thankfully, the robes she wore covered most of his love bites. And when aroused by the lovely Shirley, he did enjoy unleashing his fangs.

Shirley moaned and drew Donovan closer, but a sharp rap on her door pulled them back to reality. She blinked, as if to wipe the sensual haze from her mind.

Then her secretary called, "Judge? Time for court. And time to send hubba-hubba hubby on his way."

Regret filled Shirley's eyes. "Unfortunately, I . . ."

Donovan kissed her soundly. "No worries, my darling. Tomorrow you'll be mine, all mine. At least in the human world." As he walked away, he sang in his rich, melodious voice, "I'm getting married in the morning . . ."

CHAPTER TWO: WEDDING JITTERS

Shirley gazed into the dressing room mirror. This was her day. The day she married the man she truly loved. At least in the human world. Some might say he was too old for her. After all, he was over three hundred to her thirty-two. Fortunately, her hot, sexy husband didn't look a day over thirty-five, the year he had chosen to stop the aging process. While humans wasted billions on the search for a Fountain of Youth, born or pure-blood vampires were able to choose the day they stopped aging. It was a process Shirley didn't quite understand, but his parents had stopped aging at sixty, and his sister at thirty-eight. When Shirley completed her forced turning, she would never age past thirty-two.

While she would be the envy of her friends, Shirley was well aware that eventually, she would be unable to disguise her inability to age. Donovan had been forced to move almost every ten years, and now she would be forced to join him. The thought of starting over continuously was daunting, but necessary if they were to keep their true nature under wraps. Perhaps one day humans would accept vampires in their midst, but as a judge, Shirley had learned that humans had a huge capacity for intolerance. It was rife in their civilization. First, it was educated women and people of color. And then, while those two groups continued to struggle, certain genders, sexual preferences, disabilities, and income classes became objects of discrimination, scorn, and disdain. Humankind could not accept their own. How could they be expected to welcome other species?

Shirley shook her head and sighed. Vampires were guilty of intolerance as well. Non-pure blood vampires were called *half breeds* and treated poorly. She would face that same disrespect. And women. Well, women weren't protected at all, not like in the human world. While vampires had evolved physically and genetically, they had not evolved sociologically. They still believed women were inferior intellectually. They mandated that women should blindly submit. Not a single woman had ever served on the Vampire Coalition, their governing body. Donovan's sister, Marilyn, an appeals court judge in the human world, had been permitted to fill in for Donovan while he pretended to recover from an attack by a serial killer, but her opinions had been given no credence. They had been outright ignored.

Shirley smiled to herself. Donovan's sister was a firecracker. She had purposely stopped the aging process three years after Donovan so she would be his elder—after a life as his younger sister. And she was determined to shatter the glass ceiling in the vampire world, even though it was considered *unladylike*.

Shirley intended to be right beside her. She was fortunate to be marrying someone more supportive of women. Shirley knew Donovan would fight at her side for her rights and those of other female vamps. He was a gifted lawyer, someone who swayed juries and judges with his keen intelligence and golden tongue. Together, they would help move the Vampire World into the Twenty-First Century.

Gwendolyn Trait, Donovan's mother, appeared behind her. "My dear, you seem worlds away. Second thoughts?"

Shirley snorted. "Never. Human or not, vampire or not, Donovan is my destiny. And I am ready for whatever the future holds."

Gwendolyn nodded. "I imagine you are thinking of your parents. A wedding is one of the times you want your mother at your side and your father to give you away. 'Tis a shame they left your world so soon." Donovan's mother, who shared her son's steel-blue eyes, smiled gently, her expression filled with sympathy.

Tears misted Shirley's eyes. Her parents had been killed in a car accident when she was in law school. She hadn't been there when they drew their last breath, one of her deepest regrets. Now, the pain had lessened, but she still missed them every day. Her mother's sweet smile. Her father's booming laugh. Shirley brushed at the tears that started to form. She didn't want to ruin her face. The cosmetician had spent hours applying lotions and ointments, then makeup. Shirley knew she looked good, but tears just might leave unattractive trails down her cheeks, and for Donovan, she wanted to be beautiful. Especially on this day.

She tried to smile at Gwendolyn. "I do miss them, terribly. Unfortunately, if they were here, I doubt they would be supportive of my choices. They were proud of the fact that I was to become a lawyer, but marrying a vampire would have been outside their realm of understanding." She adjusted one of the curls piled on the top of her head. "No, it is almost a relief that I do not have to hide what I have become and who I am marrying. Too many secrets, too many lies. I doubt Donovan and I would have gotten this far."

Gwendolyn tilted her head and smiled, her auburn hair and patrician features made more lovely in the soft light. "Most likely, they would have disapproved upon first sight. Donovan's reputation as a rake would have certainly raised concern. Before he met you, there was a revolving door to his bedroom. My gorgeous son is irresistible to humans, and he took advantage. He's brilliant, charming, a true gentleman. And wealthy, extremely wealthy. Every woman's and some men's fantasy." She shook her head. "Jonathan and I were certain he would never settle down. I, for one, will be forever grateful that you finally captured his heart. You have changed him. There is a light in him now. He is excited about his future. You did that, my dear."

Shirley adjusted her veil. "That goes both ways. I have always been different, and treated differently, just because I looked like a bubble-headed blonde. All my life people have acted as if I didn't have a brain. Even in court, some still do. When I was in law school, my tax professor repeatedly called me a *dumb blonde*. He never said it in front of others, only when I went into his office to ask a question or challenge a grade. But those words hurt, and they affected how I viewed myself. Too bad the old coot died before I became a judge." She sighed. "But Donovan, he saw me for me. He never questioned my intelligence or capacity for the law. He treats me like a woman, but a woman with a brain."

Gwendolyn chuckled. "It helps that his sister is a judge. If he had displayed even a hint of misogyny, she would have flayed him with a bull whip."

"Still, Donovan is my dream man. The only man in my fantasies. The man I thought *was* a fantasy. I never believed I would find anyone who fit me so completely." Shirley smiled. "And now I am about to become his wife. For eternity."

Donovan and Shirley bowed their heads and tried to avoid the birdseed being tossed at them. They had invited only two hundred to their human wedding, but the press and many of Donovan's fans had gathered outside the church. Some women were weeping, others were cheering. And someone had given them bags of birdseed. It was raining down on their heads like a hailstorm.

"Ye Gods," Donovan muttered. "What the heck is wrong with humans? That seed stinks like bird poop. And I'm going to be removing it from my shorts for days."

Shirley giggled. "My poor darling. Does birdseed offend your vampire senses?" She patted his arm. "Since my sniffer isn't yet up to snuff, it's the pelting of my skin that annoys me. Let's get to the limousine so you can help me remove the seed from what I'm wearing under this dress."

To the delight of those assembled, Donovan scooped Shirley into his arms and ran to their transport.

Shirley giggled, her eyes illuminated with joy. "Hurry, husband. This seed is starting to itch." She wiggled her body in his arms.

Donovan chuckled. "I will see what I can do about that. It is my duty as your husband to ensure your comfort at all times." He grinned and kissed her.

The chauffeur opened the back door to the limousine and Donovan gently set Shirley on the seat. Then he ran around the vehicle, flung open the door, and dove in beside her.

Shirley snuggled up to Donovan and kissed him. "Look at it this way. Bird seed is far less dangerous than a gun. And only a few months ago, there was a gunman . . . er woman, who had us both in her sights. We could still be fearing for our lives if she hadn't run off to Switzerland. Instead, we got married peacefully, without incident." Shirley ran a finger along the waistband of Donovan's pants and dipped a finger inside.

Donovan gasped. "My dear wife, what on Earth?"

Shirley chuckled and shrugged. "Looking for birdseed, of course. I won't have my husband twitching like a skeleton on speed at the celebration of our marriage. People might think . . ." She laughed. "Well, you know. That you had ants in your pants." She giggled again.

Donovan cocked his eyebrow. "Ants in my pants? You humans are so strange. Why would I have ants in my pants? I mean, how would they even get there?" He kissed her and his tongue danced with hers. "If I'm twitching, it is because I am impatient to consummate my marriage." He reached under Shirley's dress and a pleased smile crossed his face. "Or that I am anxious to see what is under this dress."

Shirley's fingers released his cummerbund, stroked the zipper to his slacks, then undid the button on his waistband and slid the zipper down. With a glance at the privacy screen that prevented the chauffeur from viewing their antics, Shirley released Donovan's cock from his shorts. Shirley curled her fingers around his length and slowly stroked. She smiled as it grew hard.

"Darling . . ." Donovan shifted in the seat. "I don't think . . ."

Shirley leaned forward and hit a red button on the console. "Driver, please take the scenic route to the Metropolitan Club. My husband and I need some time to *decompress*." Upon receiving an affirmative response, Shirley gathered the skirt of her white princess gown and slid to her knees. She grasped her husband's male member and ran her tongue around it, then dried her saliva with her hot breath.

Donovan moaned, and gently pulled her head closer, careful not to disrupt her elegantly sculpted up-do. "Shirley . . ."

"Focus, Donovan. We're on a tight schedule." She continued to stroke his cock with her fingers and tongue while he squirmed. Then she opened her mouth and took him in—all the way in.

His eyes hooded and his vampire instincts unleashed, Donovan regarded his wife with a passion he could no longer squelch. He felt his temperature rise from its normal eighty-two degrees Fahrenheit and finally, he gave in to the intense ecstasy invading his mind. The euphoria unleashed his fangs, but he fought the urge to grab the women he loved, and imbed them in her neck. Even in the heat of the moment, he knew bite marks would raise eyebrows at their wedding reception. Lawyers had raised gossip to an art form, and even the mildest of comments would be sure to reach the ears of the media covering the event. That was not a chance he wished to take. He would not embarrass his wife.

A decisive shudder raced through his body and Donovan mumbled, "Shirley, I think I am going to . . ."

Shirley hollowed out her cheeks and sucked harder.

Donovan emitted an ungentlemanly bellow and exploded in her mouth. As his seed flowed, she drank, and drank, never once releasing her lips from his cock. When Shirley lapped up the last drop, Donovan collapsed against the fine leather seat of the limousine, his fangs exposed, just itching to bite his bride.

Shirley peered up at him, a coy smile gracing her face. Careful not to harm her gown, she rose to her feet and sat down beside him.

Donovan sat up, blinked hard, then grinned. "That was some performance, wife."

Shirley opened the petite purse she carried and pulled out a mirror and a tube of lipstick. Carefully, she smoothed her makeup, adjusted her hair, and recolored her lips. With a loud smack, she blew a kiss at her mirror and turned to Donovan. "My pleasure, darling," she cooed.

Donovan slid his arm around her shoulders and drew her close. He nuzzled her neck and his fangs nipped at an earlobe. "There is nothing more beautiful than my wife's face after she has given me pleasure, except for the expression on her face after I give her pleasure." Donovan slowly inched up her gown until he reached her waist. He gazed at the luxurious pink satin corset, the white stockings, and the non-existent panties." "Oh, wife, how you tease." His finger brushed her mound. "Don't be surprised if I haul you off the dance floor into a room with a locked door and overwhelm you with my affection."

Just as Shirley moaned her interest, the chauffeur's voice

filled their space. "Three minutes out, folks. Is it a go or would you like to continue your, uh, tour?"

Donovan groaned and sat back, smoothing down Shirley's gown. His fangs retreated. He pushed the button on the console and said, "Take us to the Metropolitan, please. I imagine I have a lifetime to ravish my wife."

Shirley giggled. "Why do you always sound British after you've achieved the *big O?*" In a mock posh British accent, she cooed, "You sound so *veddy, veddy* proper." She adjusted his cummerbund, then his slacks. "Thank God, you're not." She growled. "My husband is an animal." Her laugh was loud and scintillating.

Donovan grinned. *And she's all mine.*

Chapter Three: Oops!

Donovan tapped his foot impatiently. He was married to Shirley in the human world. Why did they have to get married again just to satisfy a bunch of old vampires? Forcing her to submit to a longer and even more bizarre ritual felt like overkill, but what the Vampire Coalition demanded, they got. Donovan was a member of the Coalition. You'd think they would give him a pass or *something*. If Shirley hadn't undergone a forced turning, she probably would have thrown up her hands and walked away.

"This reminds me of my nuptials." Jonathan Trait clapped his son, Donovan, on the shoulder. "Though your mother has added a few more touches. We had a string quartet. She seems to have assembled an orchestra." His hand swept the expanse of the Grand Vampire Legion Hall. "This is amazing."

Donovan chuckled. "She wanted a gospel choir, but Shirley convinced her that wasn't necessary."

Jonathon nodded. "Shirley also put the kibosh on the horse and carriage, a royal litter, and a throne. Your wife does not have a pretentious bone in her body. She allowed your mother a little leeway, but she insisted on simplicity. I am surprised your mother agreed."

"Well, she did allow Mother to bring in a swing band for the reception and a salsa band for the afterparty."

"But she nixed the celebrity chef and insisted on a local one. A human."

Donovan snorted. "Whose memory will be wiped clean as soon as the celebration ends. He will think he catered a party for Chicago's inner circle, nothing more."

"Well, it's not like we will be flashing our fangs or feasting on humans. Our ceremony will be long and, to outsiders, tedious. It's a good thing humans are excluded. I am quite sure they would not understand Shirley's coronation." Jonathan removed a gold pocket watch from his vest. "I have been waiting for the physician's report to present to the rest of the Coalition. The wedding can't proceed without a proper license."

Donovan cocked an eyebrow. "Still? I thought that was to be completed this morning."

"The physician wanted to run some more tests. He was worried about the side effects from the turning."

Donovan paled. "Did he think Shirley was ill?"

His father shook his head. "No, nothing like that. I think Shirley reported feeling a little light-headed, that's all. I would suspect it's all the excitement."

"Maybe I should go to her . . ."

Jonathan grabbed his arm. "Don't you dare. I am under strict orders to keep you away from the bride. Your mother would have my head."

"But if she is ill . . ."

"We would have heard by now."

A messenger rushed into the room carrying a large envelope. He handed it to Jonathan. "From Doctor Littleton, My Lord."

Jonathan bowed stiffly. "Please thank the good doctor for me."

The messenger scurried away. Jonathan opened the envelope and reviewed the report. When he got to the last page, his eyes grew wide. "Donovan, it seems Shirley had a reason for that lightheadedness."

Donovan gasped. "What is it?"

His father handed him the document and pointed at the bottom of the page. "She's pregnant."

Donovan grabbed at the wall. Overwhelmed with unfamiliar emotion, he settled onto a chair and rested his head in his hands. "Ye Gods," he muttered. "I'm going to be a father."

"And I am to be a grandfather, finally. However, I am afraid the Coalition may have a problem with this. They may not permit your marriage today or anytime soon."

Donovan Trait turned to his father, his eyes filled with fury. "Why does it matter? We're already married in the human world and we are about to repeat our vows before all in the Vampire Kingdom. This doesn't change anything. It's not like we are going to have a child out of wedlock. We have broken no laws."

Jonathan Trait arched a fluffy white brow. "We need to discuss this, son." He sat beside him. "The problem is you explicitly agreed to allow the Coalition to oversee the conception and birth of any children born of this joining. Every step of the process was to be observed, studied, and documented. You know this."

"So, they are going to force us to terminate the pregnancy and start over?" Donovan groaned. "It's too late. I will not force her to start over. They can be *voyeurs* the next time. I am sure Shirley will have no problem with the monitoring of her pregnancy. It's not like she can consult with a human physician. They would not understand that her child may have fangs in utero. And the blood work . . ." He shuddered. "I can't imagine what . . ."

Jonathan frowned. "The agreement says from the point of conception, son. You know what sticklers they are. Our women became barren more than a century ago. We need to understand why. From a scientific perspective, we need to know exactly what was different, so we can find a solution."

Donovan harrumphed. "Seriously? Did they wish to observe while I made love to my wife? That's ludicrous. Horny old bastards."

Jonathan chuckled. "Some of those old fuddie-duddies would stroke out if forced to watch a virile man like you seduce his wife." His expression turned somber. "Let's look at the facts as we know them. As a lawyer, that's a process with which you are familiar.

"Human women can't carry a vampire child to term. We know that. They miscarry. The human uterus is simply not strong enough to withstand the damage caused by a developing vampire fetus. Those fangs shred the amniotic sac. However, we also don't know if a female vampire can carry a human baby to term. Shirley may not be able to provide the fetus with the nutrition that it needs to develop properly.

"In addition, we don't know the point of conception, which means we don't know if Shirley was fully turned when she conceived. We also don't know what the genetic makeup of the baby will be and whether that will change as the pregnancy progresses. Furthermore, we don't know whether the baby's genetics will alter after birth. We don't know what the child will need to survive. We don't know much.

"That raises several questions, Donovan. Is Shirley's life in danger? And is your child's life in danger? Not just physically and genetically, but socially. The baby is an anomaly. To some, an abomination. A freak. He or she will constantly be in danger. If you had kept to the agreement, she and the baby would have been protected. Now everything is at risk."

Donovan paled. He choked out, "Bloody hell, this child is a miracle. A pure defiance of medicine. You can't seriously believe the Coalition would destroy my child. Force Shirley to . . ."

Jonathan sighed heavily. "This situation will terrify them. It's a huge risk. They can't handle the unknown. They will always take the easy path. You and I have tried to pull them into the Twenty-First Century, and they have fought us every step of the way. I fear this may be our last stand. They have no respect for miracles." Jonathan finger-combed his thick white hair. His light green eyes revealed his concern. "To them, conception is nothing more than a scientific process."

Donovan's eyes misted. Vampires lived for centuries. Unfortunately, that did not make them any more intelligent. In fact, vampires were frightened of change, anything that deviated from the norm. They had little thirst for knowledge because they felt they knew it all. They had been forced to evolve as the human world changed, but many still choose to self-terminate rather than adapt.

He and Shirley had consented to a grand experiment. Shirley's eggs had been extracted at each stage of the turning so scientists could determine what was preventing conception in vampire women. Her eggs would be mated with Donovan's sperm in a test tube to determine when or if Shirley's fertility was impaired in the turning process. Any viable embryos would be saved for implantation throughout their long lives. They had observed all birth control practices. The conception that occurred was an accident. It should not be treated as a crime.

Donovan swiped at his eyes. Dammit. *Vampires don't cry.* Most were incapable of emotion. Since falling in love with sweet Shirley, however, many emotions had risen to the surface and laid him bare. "Well, Father, I think we have a choice to make. Do we tell the Coalition of Shirley's pregnancy and risk all of the horrible things you have predicted? Or do I go through with the marriage, keep Shirley secluded until the baby is born, enact measures to protect both my wife and child and face the Coalition's wrath then?"

His father rolled his eyes. "I am grateful vamps can only tell if *humans* are lying. Otherwise, I would not survive an inquisition by those old goats." He shook his head "I stand with you and Shirley, no matter what you two decide. However, this is primarily Shirley's decision. Her body is her own, and thus, she must determine how to proceed."

"Then I say we keep quiet until forced to speak. No one has the right to harm my wife or my unborn child — in the human or the vampire worlds. We will tell the Coalition when forced, not a minute before. Meanwhile, this marriage will proceed as planned. Give them the report, minus the last page. They will never know the difference.

"We have come too far. Shirley has sacrificed too much. It's my job to protect her and my child, and I shall."

Shirley stared at herself in the large makeup mirror. First she had been pampered to the point of exhaustion. Then she had been subjected to a myriad of grooming techniques, from a mani-pedi to a rather unpleasant removal of body hair. When she had joked about the possibility of waxing her scalp, the technician had appeared interested. Shirley shuddered. The technician had been stoic and firm, her personality teetering on cruel. When she ripped off those strips of wax and Shirley screamed, the technician had tried to hide a smile. Clearly, the woman was a sadist.

If her mother-in-law, Gwendolyn, had not been present, Shirley was sure the situation would have grown even more unpleasant. She shifted uncomfortably in her chair. She felt like she had been encased in a tent of brocade. Already she was perspiring. Could the vapors be far behind?

Gwendolyn Trait studied her and smiled. "You look glorious, dear. A princess truly worthy of a Vampire Prince."

Shirley blushed. Her turning had paled her complexion slightly, but as a natural blonde with a strong Swedish heritage, she was already light-complected. A blush had always stood out. However, at that moment, it clashed with the elaborate jewel-colored gown she wore. Shirley made a face at herself in the makeup mirror. "I feel like a gaudy peacock in a gaggle of elegant swans. I mean, this dress is really too much. It must weigh hundreds of pounds. I'm not sure I can walk in it." She blushed again. "I don't mean to insult you, Gwendolyn, but it's a wedding. I would think the gown I wore in my human ceremony would do."

Gwendolyn waved her hand. "It would clash with that lovely crown. This is a coronation as well as a joining. You must not only play the role of a princess, but you must also wear clothing that demonstrates that status. For the first time in many centuries, new blood is coming into the Trait line. It is not only a cause for celebration but also a statement to our political enemies that we will not be deterred. I was worried that Donovan and his sister, Marilyn, would be the last of the Traits. Now there is a possibility of a new generation, and that gives us hope, Shirley. It's a wonderful feeling. Hope." She clapped her hands, an expression of delight crossing her face. "That dress makes it clear who and what we are celebrating. Continuity."

Shirley patted her hair. The stylists had spent hours washing, then combing and fashioning an elaborate up-do. All that was required was a crown. She had seen it. It was the very definition of ostentatious. As a just-turned vampire, Shirley knew it wasn't her place to object, but gosh darn it, her friends in the human world would collapse in fits and giggles. It was a good thing humans weren't allowed at this celebration. It was certainly over the top. *Way* over the top.

Still, Shirley couldn't help but wonder how her long-deceased parents would have felt about this marriage. Both had been teachers, one high school, the other middle school. Would they have reacted with horror at marriage to a vampire? Would she have been permitted to disclose it? Would they react with curiosity, then celebrate the fact that she had found her soulmate, her forevermore? She sighed. Her parents had not had a prejudiced bone in their bodies. They had been accepting of all races, genders, and cultures. As teachers, that had almost been required. They had passed that tolerance on to their daughter. Perhaps that why she had been able to accept all the changes in her life.

Yes, she loved Donovan Trait unconditionally. And now, eternally. As a born human, as a now-turned vampire. Without the slightest bit of hesitation. Shirley sighed deeply and gently rubbed her stomach. She just hoped she wasn't coming down with the flu. Did vampires even get the flu? She had felt ill during breakfast, and a bit light-headed while racing around preparing for the ceremony. Ginger ale helped, but the last thing she wanted to do was faint in front of thousands of vampires. That would only give them further reason to cast aspersions on a half- breed, a human turned.

A wave of nausea swept through her and Shirley moaned.

"Oh, dear." Gwendolyn hurriedly grabbed a small trash bin and set it next to Shirley's chair. "I do hope you aren't coming down with something. Unless . . ." She gazed at Shirley and smiled. "Unless I can expect to hear the pitter-patter of little feet soon."

Shirley expelled a heavy breath. "Not a chance. On the orders of the Coalition, I have been rendered infertile for the near future. It's bad enough I was once human. God forbid Donovan's child carry any of those human genes." Her face mocked a stern expression. "A vampire prince cannot father a half-breed."

Donovan paced the length of the Grand Vampire Legion Hall.

To onlookers, he appeared to be a nervous groom. In reality, he was worried about Shirley. His attempts to converse with her had been blocked by his mother and sister. How typical of them to adopt a human myth when it suited them. It was it bad luck for a groom to see his bride on their wedding day? Who made that stuff up? It was ridiculous.

Finally, he returned to the stage and sat in one of the throne-like chairs set in the middle. Perhaps it was best to wait — when they were alone and away from others. The honeymoon was the perfect time to share his happy but yet distressing news. Donovan straightened the many medals and ribbons affixed to his elegant tuxedo. He wore them sparingly. They signified his rank in the Vampire World. He also wore a crown on his head. The darn thing was heavy and more than a little annoying.

Donovan wasn't a fan of pomp and circumstance. When living in the UK, it was more acceptable. In America, however, it just seemed extreme. This country had fought to be free of a king. Over the centuries, he had discovered that he much preferred a kingless world. He often wished that the Vampire Kingdom would eliminate their monarchy so he could just be a wealthy lawyer. With no royal responsibility.

Of course, part of his mother's insistence on this ceremony was due to the emotional fallout after his family was deprived of its royal lineage in the human world. When his grandfather was turned, the royal family had been appalled and cast him out. Apparently, his blood was no longer royal. It was tainted. His grandfather was removed from the line of succession as if he had never existed, stripped of all titles and holdings.

The Vampire Kingdom had grudgingly welcomed his grandfather into their ranks and provided some recognition of his lineage. As the kingdom grew, it was clear that some sort of hierarchy would be required if their species were to survive. His grandfather and several other turned military and political types banded together and brokered deals with vampire tribes and settlements. The governing Vampire Coalition was born.

After his grandfather lost his wife to the human flu pandemic in the early nineteen hundreds — she drank tainted blood out of desperation and did not seek care until it was too late — he self-terminated, and Jonathan Trait assumed his seat on the Coalition. Donovan was added to the Coalition when it became clear a skilled lawyer was needed to assist with adapting laws to a rapidly changing human world. So many vamps lived in the human world, and the restrictions imposed by the Coalition had made it difficult to function without raising suspicion. Vampires had to blend in with humans, not stand out.

Donovan tapped impatiently on the arm of his chair. He was anxious to unite with Shirley in the Vampire World. Though she had claimed her wedding among humans was sufficient, Donovan had insisted. He wanted her afforded all of the privileges of his status as a prince and pure-blood, and the only way to do that was to bond in a centuries old ritual.

A piano and cello began to play *Canon in D* by Pachelbel. Members of the Coalition, dressed in morning coats and other finery entered the hall. More instruments joined in, increasing the potency of the music, building to a glorious crescendo. The elders entered, their stoic expressions worthy of such a momentous occasion. When they had settled around a long table on one side of the stage, the orchestra launched into Handel's *The King Shall Rejoice,* originally written for the coronation of George II, shortly after the Traits had been cast out from the British Royal Family.

Donovan watched with pride as his sister, Marilyn, and his mother escorted Shirley down the long aisle, their arms entwined. They walked slowly and proudly, each a glowing visage of vampire womanhood. Marilyn was dressed in a simple blue gown, a glittering tiara atop her tight mahogany curls. And his mother, Gwendolyn, wore an elegant green dress, the hem embroidered with the colors in Shirley's dress, a symbol of her acceptance of Shirley into the Trait family. Gwendolyn also wore a many-jeweled crown that glowed in the lights of the overhead chandeliers.

But it was Shirley who most drew his attention. She was resplendent in a gown that was a luminous swirl of color. It was elegant, yet vibrant, a dress that screamed of her ascendance to royalty. Her luscious blonde hair had been fashioned into a cascade of curls. All that was required was the crown. His gaze locked with hers, and Donovan felt his heart leap, his love for this woman suffusing every inch of his being. It had not been an easy road, but it had been a worthy one. Donovan had waited centuries for this moment, the day his life would meld with another for eternity. This woman filled him with a warmth that could only be described as love. She was his one love, his true love. Always.

His mother and sister led Shirley up the steps to the stage and left her standing before Donovan. The notes of Handel were extinguished, then Shirley knelt before him, her head bowed in submission. Donovan stood and lifted the crown that sat on a small table next to his chair. He held it above Shirley's head and in an ancient vampire tongue, recited the words of coronation. "Aebeli Ki Mon, Kar Delonge Althrea, Esper Danal Esper Ti, Lo Aebeli Lo Ki. Redable Le Tomori Ti, Met Cronola, Quewla, Et Maro." *Here is your future Queen, the woman of my heart. Bow to her as you bow to me. She is our destiny. May she serve you as she serves me, with humility, wisdom, and grace.*"

There was a roar of acclamation from the crowd.

Donovan lowered the crown and set it precisely upon her head. He offered Shirley his hand and gently pulled her to her feet. Shirley's eyes were bright with emotion as she gazed at him. He whispered, "I love you," then turned her toward those assembled in the hall. With a triumphant smile, Donovan proclaimed, "She is your future Queen. I give you, Princess Shirley. Long may she reign!"

The crowd broke into cheers and stomped their feet. Their approval was clear. Donovan was much loved in the Vampire

Nation. The human world saw him as a sex symbol, a lawyer with a commitment to the disadvantaged. Vampires appreciated his service on the Coalition, but they also valued his heritage.

Donovan and Shirley sat on their chairs and acknowledged the applause with a slight bow of their heads. When it died down, the orchestra began to play a solemn tune. Jonathan Trait entered, his long black robes resembling those of a priest. He stood before the couple and began to recite the history of the Vampire Nation.

He chanted with elegance, his ancient words reminding the assembly of the sanctioned tale of creation. How vampire bats first craved the blood of bovines, biting them as they slept, lapping up their blood. The tale of a simple farmer, who, seeking to protect his livestock, battled with a bat and wound up covered in bites. The melding of his blood with that of a bat transformed him into an otherworldly being, with fangs, sensitivity to light, an unquenchable thirst for blood, and most of all, supernatural powers — enhanced hearing and vision, a refined sense of taste and smell, and eternal life.

And as time passed and more humans received the bite of the bat, or a single vampire, the farmer was no longer alone. Vampires congregated in tribes and colonies, emerging only to satisfy the need to feed. They intermarried with each other, extinguishing the blood of the human and eventually producing children with pure vampire blood. Purebloods. The strongest of the strong.

For an hour, Jonathan chanted about the vampire's journey, his words at times melodic, at other times gruff. He told of the emergence of civility from chaos, the creation of ruling bodies, fair and equal governance, and the evolution of vampire science. Finally his voice grew hoarse, his words strained. As he turned the final page of the yellowed book he held, Jonathan said simply, "And so, we continue this journey." He turned and approached the Coalition. He bowed and then joined them.

Another man emerged from behind the curtains, this one dressed in white robes. He carried another ancient tome. The man approached Donovan and Shirley and began to speak. "A vampire joining is not a ritual to take lightly. It honors the path of our ancestors. It pledges one life to another for eternity. It celebrates what we have become. This journey did not begin as other journeys have. Nor will it end as other journeys did. Each of us has a destiny independent of others, and until a formal joining, that destiny is unfulfilled. 'Tis fate that brought the two of you here. 'Tis faith that binds your lives. We don't speak much of love, but instead of respect, duty, honor, and responsibility. Yet, vampires can and do love. It is not the emotion of the human world, but instead an all-encompassing sense of rightness, of comfort, of embracing fate." He gestured to Donovan and Shirley, indicating that they should stand.

He smiled at them and intoned, "Do you, Donovan and Shirley, pledge your fidelity to this nation, its people, and each other?"

Shirley and Donovan responded as one. "We do."

"Do you, Donovan and Shirley, embrace the laws and customs of this nation, for the eternity of your lives?"

"We do."

"Do you, Donovan and Shirley, vow to respect, support, and honor the person you have chosen as your life partner?"

"We do."

The man turned to those assembled. "If there is anyone in this assembly who protests this joining as a violation of our laws, speak now or forever retain your silence."

Donovan waited, his eyes rapidly scanning the crowd. He was confident no one knew of Shirley's pregnancy. The only protest would concern her origins as a human. No one moved. No one gave any indication of protest. His mother had chosen the guests wisely.

The officiant smiled. He turned back to Donovan and Shirley. "Then it is within my authority to sanction this joining. May you serve this union with wisdom, humility, devotion, and kindness." The man again turned to the crowd. "What the Vampire Nation has joined, let no vampire or man put asunder."

A trumpet ensemble assembled along the long aisle and burst into a celebratory fanfare. Donovan took Shirley's hand and they walked through the musicians' arch, the flags attached to the trumpets fluttering as they passed. Jonathon, Gwendolyn, and Marilyn followed.

All of them walked to a small room off of the hall.

Shirley hurried to a deep green loveseat and with a loud *Oomph* settled on it. Donovan attempted to sit next to her, but her voluminous gown prevented it. She giggled and tried to make room for him. After moving the skirt around, she finally stood and pointed to the furniture. "You sit. I'll perch on your lap. It's the only way. I am not about to allow a garment to prevent me from snuggling with my husband." She smiled at him lovingly.

Donovan sat and pulled her onto his lap. "Ye Gods! This is like being wrapped in a shroud. How many layers does this skirt have?" He tugged at Shirley's dress. "Will all of your gowns have all these layers from now on? I much prefer your tailored suits and dresses. This is . . ." He flushed. "Well, outrageous."

Shirley laughed, then kissed him. "I'm guessing your mother knows the answer to that. I feel like a princess, but this creation is heavy. And hot. Stifling, really. I was afraid I wouldn't make it down the aisle. It's not comfortable, at all. I need water,"

A servant poised against the wall nodded and left the

room.

"And food." Donovan gazed at a second servant. "She needs food."

The man also nodded and left.

As soon as the room was cleared of non-family members, Jonathan cleared his throat. "We have another matter to attend to."

Everyone turned to him.

Jonathan began to pace. "Donovan and I, I mean, I, did something that's likely to incur the wrath of the Coalition, and we need to be prepared for it."

Gwendolyn cocked her delicate brow. "*Everything* upsets those old coots. What did you do? Sneeze without a handkerchief at the ready?"

Marilyn laughed. "Perhaps his morning coat had a wrinkle?"

Jonathan attempted to smile, but his mouth lapsed into a frown. "I wish. This matter is much graver and it is going to shake the Vampire Nation to its very core."

Shirley gazed at him "I thought once Donovan and I married, everything would settle down . . ."

Donovan took her hand and kissed the palm. He sighed heavily. "I'm afraid there's a complication, darling. One we seem to have created."

Shirley stared at him. "What could possibly have gone wrong? We have adhered to every rule, every restriction placed upon us." Her face reddened. "I will not allow them to throw another roadblock in our way." She shook her head vigorously and tears welled in her eyes. "No, no, no. They have put us through enough. They have put *me* through enough. I am done with them. We are finally bound forever and that is that."

"Shirley, you're pregnant."

Gwendolyn squealed and Marilyn paled.

Shirley collapsed against her husband. Finally, she managed to speak. "What?"

Donovan grinned. He pointed at her. "You and I, we made a baby. The old-fashioned way."

"But we took precautions. We promised that we would hold off until . . ." Shirley choked. "Oh my God, we're in deep doo-doo. The Coalition, they're going to flip." She grabbed Donovan's face by the ears and kissed him soundly. "To hell with them. Darling, we're going to have a baby. A little vampire or vampette. That's wonderful." She paused and giggled. "Which is why I have been feeling so nauseous. I'm pregnant. I'm so happy." She kissed Donovan again.

Jonathan held up his hand. "And in violation of the agreement made between you and the Coalition. Some of them are going to be out for blood. They are going to think you conceived on purpose. That this was intentional. They could intervene in the ugliest of ways."

Gwendolyn scoffed. "What could they do? She's fully vampire now."

Marilyn rose and began to pace. "Ye Gods, this is awful. They could ruin everything. Those bastards are vicious when crossed. They don't trust humans. They will believe this was intentional." Like the judge that she was, she stopped in front of Donovan and Shirley and drew herself up. She glared at them. "You are so fucked. In addition to the legal repercussions, there are health risks. On the one hand, the Coalition could allow the pregnancy to proceed as a matter of science. There are too many unknowns and we need answers. On the other, they may wish to punish the two of you. They could put you under house arrest, exile you, even force you to . . ." She expelled a breath. "To terminate the pregnancy."

"Over my dead body." Gwendolyn rose to her feet. Her expression was thunderous. "I have waited centuries for a grandchild, and no one is going to take that away from me."

She gestured toward Shirley. "If I have to kidnap Shirley and take her underground, I will. I have the resources. *You damn well know I do,* and I am not afraid to use them."

Marilyn joined her mother and slid an arm around her waist. "As do I. Those men have sacrificed the rights of female vampires for the last time. It's Shirley's body and her decision, and no one can take that away from her." She slanted a slight grin at her brother. "I'm sorry, Donovan, but Mother is right. This is our last stand. The one moment in time when we women have to stand together. If the Coalition even looks at Shirley the wrong way, we will disappear."

Donovan sighed. "Father and I thought it might be best to simply disappear on a year-long honeymoon and reappear after the baby is born."

Shirley stood. "Wait a minute. I'm not going anywhere. I'm not going to hide. I am carrying the child of the man I love and I am damn proud of it. I will tell them myself. This is too important." She smiled at Marilyn and Gwendolyn. "This child is a miracle, not an atrocity. Donovan and I accomplished something no one in this world has for over a century. We should be applauded, and if not, I will fight those bastards." She planted her arms on her hips. "I will bear this child. I will raise her in the vampire world. And neither my husband nor I will suffer because of it."

Shirley huffed. "No one messes with Shirley Magnusen Trait. No one."

Chapter Four: The Trial

As was their duty, Shirley and Donovan formally notified the Coalition of her pregnancy after they returned from a brief honeymoon.

When questioned further, Shirley admitted she had no idea when the pregnancy had occurred or how. As far as she was concerned, it was an accident. A rare occurrence, yes, but certainly not intentional. She had signed an affidavit to that effect, as had Donovan.

Shirley had been appalled at the swiftness with which she had been notified of the charges against her. She was grateful that she had not been arrested and taken into custody before this trial, but she had been warned that some members of the Coalition had become enraged when notified of her pregnancy. She was well aware that those vampires were capable of exceptionally punitive measures. At this very moment, as she stood before the Coalition, Shirley was certain of only one thing. She and Donovan would protect their child at all costs.

She wasn't worried about the risks to herself. Shirley was only worried about the child growing inside her.

Now she stood before the Coalition, her gaze steady and strong. She had dressed in a deep royal blue skirt suit, her power color. Donovan said it matched her eyes, but for Shirley, it was about dressing the part. She wanted to appear confident, fearless. With her blonde hair pulled back into a tidy bun, sapphire studs nestled on her earlobes, and only her wedding ring on her manicured hands, she felt invincible. As she needed to be.

There was no way she was going to allow a group of grouchy old vampires to take her down. She had been a judge long enough to know that the only way to battle a bunch of blowhards was to face them head-on. She might be a woman, but she was mighty. Her inner self agreed with a loud roar. Shirley fought to hide her smile. She and Donovan's sister had spent a week preparing for her appearance before this tribunal. They had examined the ancient tomes that ruled the vampire world meticulously. They had left no stone unturned.

Marilyn, who stood beside her as counsel, leaned over and whispered. "Don't let the old goats unnerve you. In the end, they will be old whining Billy goats."

"After a taking few nips out of me. You know how goats are. They have no restraint. They munch on anything and everything in sight."

"Thankfully they are old. They need naps. We will be out of here in an hour. Which means, of course, there will be a limit on just how much they can munch."

Shirley offered a small smile, then returned her gaze to the Coalition. All of the members were seated, including Donovan and his father. Some of these men might be out for blood, but she had to trust that those two would keep the entire group in line. While Donovan had been forced to recuse himself from the final vote, he would be permitted to engage in the proceedings and offer guidance as the Coalition's counsel.

She studied the remaining panel. It was the same group she had faced when seeking permission to marry.

Harold Hannigan, a tall, spindly man with grizzled gray hair and polished dark skin. His brown eyes remained glued to the papers set before him as if he was hesitant to acknowledge the presence of Shirley and Marilyn.

Mortimer March, who appeared to be in his mid-fifties. His dark brown hair was thick, just barely graced with gray. He was what some would call pleasantly handsome, with even features and a slight smile gracing his full lips. As if he thought the world a joke.

Alexander Holmes possessed sparse pure white hair that curled around his head at awkward angles. With wire-rimmed glasses perched on the end of his nose, he had the appearance of a mad scientist. Which he was, according to Marilyn.

Charles Bengotten, every inch the suave, debonair bachelor. His strong features were sharpened by a tight cap of well-coiffed light brown hair. At the moment, his expression was fierce, almost angry. He glared at Shirley and Marilyn, his eyes filled with rage.

It took but a moment for Shirley to identify who would be the hard sells. Hannigan and Bengotten. They would be the ones who would push for sanctions, even punishment. Their disapproval was evident.

Donovan walked to where Shirley and Marilyn stood. Facing the Coalition, then spoke with clarity and authority. "My Lords, you have called this hearing to discuss, mediate, and rule on the perceived infractions of Judge Shirley Magnusen Trait. The charges are as follows.

"We, the Coalition of the Vampire Nation, do hereby charge the defendant with the failure to adhere and conform to an agreement made June fifteenth, twenty thousand twenty, concerning the circumstances under which a child may be legally conceived between pure-blood Donovan Hastings Trait and half-breed Shirley Magnusen Trait.

"To wit, that said conception was to occur only upon the agreement of the Coalition.

"To wit, that said conception was to occur only after defendant Magnusen Trait had completed the procedure known as forced turning, as documented by Coalition-approved researchers and physicians.

"To wit, that said conception and pregnancy were to be fully documented and monitored by Coalition-approved researchers and physicians.

"As evidence exists that defendant Magnusen Trait failed to properly adhere to the provisions set forth in said agreement, and has conceived a child of indeterminant mixed origins, she is hereby charged with violation of said agreement, as well as Vampire Code, Rule Fourteen Hundred Point Two. Miscegenation. Intermarriage Among Breeds and Races, and Rule Fourteen Hundred Point Three. Paternity. Children Born of Unions Between Vampires and Other Breeds.

"By a majority vote of said Coalition, these charges shall be pleaded and tried." Donovan paused. "Allow me to state for the record that although this tribunal has stripped me of the right to vote in these proceedings, I stand with Judge Shirley Magnusen, my wife. None of the acts accused were intentional and that she has been charged is untenable."

Hannigan sneered at him. "And that is the reason you have been recused. Proceed, Lord Trait."

Donovan turned to Shirley. "Defendant Magnusen Trait, you have been availed of the charges before this esteemed council. Per the Vampire Code, your guilt is assumed as a matter of law. Do you wish to present evidence that may refute this finding?"

Shirley studied the Coalition, her gaze moving from man to man. She straightened her stance, but her lip quivered. She was so damn mad that she and Donovan had been forced into this situation. However, she was even angrier that she had been the only one charged. No, her husband had been given a pass because he was male and a true-blood vampire. That discrimination rankled. It would never fly in the human world. Now, she almost wished she still was one. A human, that was. Shirley forced her might into her voice. "I state unequivocally and unconditionally that I will fight these charges until I take my last breath. They are born of an ancient and misogynist code that has no place in today's world. They are an insult to me, my mate, and turned vampires everywhere." She pointed a finger at the Coalition, her anger now apparent in the trembling of that digit. "How dare you mount this ridiculous mockery of the law? You should be ashamed. Each and every one of you should be ashamed."

Marilyn grabbed her arm and whispered, "Enough. Let us try this as humans do. With dignity and respect. These men don't respond to emotion, they denigrate it. Mind your tongue."

Shirley nodded and settled into the chair provided. Her pregnancy hormones were all over the place and her caution had abated. Her response to being with child mirrored those of humans. If she wasn't crying, she was raging. Most vamps had been given centuries of training to control their emotions. She had not.

A pained expression crossed Donovan's face. He had been devastated by the charges. Yet he was the one who held her each night as she wept over the fate of her child. He was the one who understood the injustice waged. Despite his many centuries of experience with human law, he was now forced to subject the fate of his wife and child to archaic vampire rules. It was a cruel fate and in human terms, unacceptable, but in the vampire world, fair. As a member of the Coalition and its legal counselor, he was bound to enforce vampire law. He had to trust Shirley and Marilyn could force the Coalition to see reason.

Yet, Donovan was not the one who felt the tiny flutters of life in the belly. Or the nausea that came as the child within her grew and gained strength by drawing on the resources within her body. He was not the one who had bonded with their child the minute her egg was implanted with his seed. She had created and was sustaining life. It was a task for women only—something not a single member of the Coalition could ever biologically experience.

Intellectually, Donovan might know what was at stake. But he would never understand the devastating impact this trial could have on a woman's mind, heart, and soul. The loss of this child—whether intentionally or unintentionally—would kill her.

Donovan's eyes softened as he said with daunting formality, "Let the record show that the defendant, Shirley Magnusen Trait, has declared her intention to refute the charges as read." His gaze shifted to Marilyn. "Counselor, you may proceed."

Marilyn stood and strode to the podium. She gently placed a folder on the stand and gazed at the men assembled. Her expression was one of challenge. A cool, almost aloof smile touched her lips, then quickly disappeared. She folded her hands and rested them on the podium. Her voice was forceful, dramatic. "I would like to thank this esteemed Coalition for the opportunity to barter for the life of the first child to be born into the Vampire Nation in more than one hundred years. It is an occasion that should be celebrated, yet you have defused any joy with your avalanche of derision, condemnation, and outright bigotry. As my client said, you should be ashamed."

The men who judged her and her client shifted uncomfortably in their chairs. Bengotten glared at her and began to speak.

Marilyn held up her hand. "I believe I am permitted to speak for ten minutes without interruption and I intend to use every single second. Please observe the rules as you have written them."

Bengotten frowned but conceded. "Proceed."

"Thank you, My Lord." Marilyn opened the folder, examined the papers within, then pushed them away. "Now as I was saying, this Coalition, in fact, the entire nation, has displayed a severe lack of civility concerning my client's pregnancy, when they should be rejoicing. While the conception itself may not have occurred in strict conformance with the agreement between the parties, the fact it occurred at all is a miracle." She shook her head. "I have to respectfully ask, why are you punishing this woman? She has done everything requested of her. Yes, to you, the conception was an unforgivable accident, but it was an accident."

"Let me begin by pointing out that my client did not violate our laws regarding miscegenation. Vampire Code, Rule Fourteen Hundred Point Two. Miscegenation. This provision clearly prohibits intermarriage among breeds and other races without the consent of the Coalition, unless otherwise governed by a treaty. When she legally joined with her husband, our physicians determined she was fully vampire. That was what was required by this Coalition, and she respected and fully complied with that provision. This was not a human and vampire joining, it was a bilateral vampire joining."

Shirley took a deep breath. The charges under the miscegenation law had made no sense. It was almost as if they were claiming she wasn't fully vampire because her turning had been performed chemically.

Marilyn aimed a controller at a whiteboard mounted on the wall. "Some of you may feel a chemical turning does not create a *real* vampire. I am well aware of those who believe a medical turning does not fully remove humanness. In fact, some call chemically-turned humans *half-breeds*." Marilyn clucked her tongue and shook her head. "Just as humans cling to myths about vampires, apparently vampires also cling to half-truths. Allow me to present the findings of our researchers."

She clicked the remote and two different DNA helixes appeared on the screen. "On the left, is human DNA. On the right, vampire DNA." She clicked the remote again and a third DNA helix was added. "This is the DNA of a chemically-turned vampire. I ask you, which helix is it most similar to?" Marilyn moved the third helix over the vampire one. They matched perfectly. "Genetically, there is no difference between the natural-born vampire and one chemically turned. A turned vampire may not immediately share the same characteristics as a born vampire, but they do have the genetic material necessary to develop them. However, our scientists also made an upgrade. They removed the gene *defect* linked to blood lust, negating the necessity for the infusion of human blood. In addition, it is our deoxyribonucleic acid that contains the additional genetic material that enhances our senses, our physical abilities, our physical assets, and our intellect. That is all present in a turned human. While vampires cannot practically become human — we cannot remove the genes that make us vampire — we have proven that those genes can be inserted into humans to make them a vampire." Marilyn smiled and arched an eyebrow. "In fact, the two helixes on the screen are those of my client and her husband. Obviously, they are a match in more ways than one."

Marilyn clicked her device, and a fourth helix appeared. "By treaty, vampires are permitted to merge with Weres. However, as we know, Weres cannot be turned. Their DNA sequencing is vastly different than ours. And while there has not been a single instance of a Were and a vampire producing a child, we have anecdotal evidence that humans and vampires can conceive children.

"Based on this evidence, alone, I have to ask, why are unions between Weres and vampires permitted, when unions with humans are not? Yes, there are claims that a human cannot safely carry a vampire fetus, that the life of the mother and child would be extinguished. But we have no real proof. Just a long-held belief that it is true. If we are indeed committed to injecting new blood into our Nation, shouldn't our first priority be to explore the viability of procreation between a vampire and turned human? I find it difficult to believe that with all of our vast medical knowledge, we are unable to ensure no harm comes to the mother and child.

"Clearly, this law makes no sense. It has crippled this Nation." Marilyn gazed at each member of the Coalition. "Our hatred of humans accumulated over time, especially in those centuries when vampires were actively hunted. However, that was a time when vampires were required to feed on humans to survive, so we had to take risks that are no longer necessary. Our science has evolved. Unfortunately, our time-bound prejudices have not. If we are being honest with ourselves, the human world could save us. They provide the best DNA match. With a few tweaks, their chromosomal material could be made to match our own.

"Have we permitted unfounded hatred, irrelevant but ever-present racism, to take precedence over the common good?"

Marilyn paused. She directed her attention to her notes, allowing the Coalition to consider her words.

Shirley watched as members of the Coalition gazed at each other. Some cocked an eyebrow in question, others whispered. It seemed as if Marilyn's arguments were getting through. Hope surged within her. *Yes.* If even half of them voted to override this ancient law, she and Donovan could live without fear of further legal retribution.

Marilyn cleared her throat. She took a sip of water from a glass that had been set at a small table beside the podium. Then she lifted her head and continued to speak. "Now, let us turn our consideration to Rule Fourteen Hundred Point Three. Paternity. Children Born of Unions Between Vampires and Other Breeds. Again, this law has been modified to favor Weres—who are not even genetically compatible—ignoring the one group who presents the greatest possibility of success for procreation—humans. Yet, our survival, our vitality, depends on our ability to procreate.

"As humans like to say, we are cutting off our noses to spite our faces. We not only prohibit unions between humans and vampires, but we also prohibit procreation between two of the most compatible species. Scientifically, that simply has no merit. If it is prejudice or fear that holds us back, we are indeed a very imprudent species.

"However, in this case, this law does not even apply. To the best of our knowledge, at the time of conception, the plaintiff *was* a vampire. Not human. While her origins were human, she underwent a complete genetic transformation by chemical means. Study her DNA helix. She is a vampire. There is no other test for vampire traits. That's it. She is fully vampire.

"However, your argument is that we cannot specifically pinpoint the time of conception, that the child may not be fully vampire. Please, enlighten me. The child is at least four-fifths, if not more vampire. Why isn't that enough? The majority of the required genetic material has been transferred to the fetus. Our scientists say if anything, the child's body will treat any extraneous human genes as recessive traits. Present, but unlikely to emerge.

"I know our scientists and physicians are disappointed that they could not monitor the point of conception to determine what variances made it possible. However, since the plaintiff has willingly agreed to be a Guinea pig for the Vampire Nation and this Coalition, *what is the problem?*

"Is your argument truly that she violated the letter of the law? Because she did not do so intentionally, in fact, she strictly adhered to your restrictions. She honored the agreement to the best of her ability. She cannot explain how this pregnancy occurred, nor can our scientists. It is an unknown, and if it is unknown, how can guilt be implied? Is it because she was once human? Is it because you wish to strike a blow against the Traits? Please, enlighten me.

"For a criminal charge to be proven, you first must have proof of intent. You must irrefutably prove that the defendant intended to violate this provision of this Code. I respectfully submit that is proof you do not have. At all times, my client behaved appropriately and with the requirements of the Coalition at the forefront of mind. You cannot prove otherwise."

Marilyn gripped the edges of the podium and slowly lifted her eyes to gaze at the Coalition. "So, I can only conclude that the motive behind these charges is not about justice, or even to abate a threat to the Vampire Nation. I must conclude that there is another reason. An improper one. My Lords, we can debate the rightness of these laws or we can face facts. The Vampire Nation is entrenched in a time warp. We have failed to adapt those laws to changing times. I can respect tradition, we are steeped in it, but we cannot permit tradition to hold us back, to prevent progress and necessary change. If we are to survive, we must evolve. If we are to evolve, we must change. We have no choice.

"In conclusion, I respectfully submit to you that my plaintiff is guilty of no crime. She has violated no law. She has complied with all of our laws and your agreements to the best of her ability. And in so doing, she presented our world with a miracle. One we so desperately need. Study her. Learn from her. Rejoice in her. Do not wrongfully penalize her. More importantly, do not force her to terminate this pregnancy."

A soft buzzer sounded, indicating the end of her allowed time to speak. Marilyn grabbed her folder and sat down next to Shirley.

Shirley gazed at her with pride. "You said everything I would have said and more."

Marilyn took a deep breath. "Let's see if they agree."

After an hour of questioning witnesses, the Coalition finally adjourned to discuss Shirley's fate.

CHAPTER FIVE: FLIGHT

Shirley sipped on purple grape juice, the replacement for her favorite glass of wine, a full-bodied Malbec. It was a concession she had made upon learning of her pregnancy. She would do nothing to harm this child.

It was almost a relief that she would soon learn of her fate. She had thought it silly when Marilyn insisted she dress in pregnancy jeans and a large grey hoodie, with her hair hidden in a dark cap. But the longer they waited for the Coalition's decision, the more anxious she became. She wanted to believe the Coalition would see reason, but if their motives were suspect, as Marilyn believed, her primary allegiance was to her child and Donovan. She would not hesitate to flee.

Marilyn paced in front of the sliding glass doors that faced the garden. Her mother-in-law, Gwendolyn, sat stiffly in an armchair, stabbing impatiently at needlework. Shirley gazed at them with fondness. Donovan's family had stepped up and supported her with everything they had. Unfortunately, if forced to disappear, she and Donovan would be separated from them for a long time. They had not even disclosed where they would exile. Plausible deniability was best. However, if they fled, it was their family who would pay.

The burner phone that permitted Donovan to communicate with her untraced chimed. Shirley ran to pick it up, but Marilyn was faster. She swiped the screen and her face paled. "Dammit. You've been acquitted on count one, but convicted on count two. Sentencing will be tomorrow. You've been put under house arrest." Her voice shook with rage. "I am turning in my vampire card. I no longer wish to be a part of this world. I will not continue to suffer those fools. *This* . . . is war." She waved at Shirley. "You must flee."

Shirley flung herself at Gwendolyn and hugged her tightly. Then she hugged Marilyn. Shirley knew that vampires didn't feel much emotion, but somehow even after turning, Shirley's had remained intact. Perhaps that was the result of her pregnancy — it had been so long since a female vampire carried a child that there was no real information — but Shirley already felt the loss of the only family she had. Marilyn gently pushed her toward the sliding doors that led through the garden. "Go with grace. Remember, they will meet you at the Old Water Tower. They have everything you will need."

Shirley pulled the hood of her sweatshirt over her head and ran through the garden to a little-used alley in the back. There an old yellow cab idled. Shirley ran to it and slipped inside.

The driver turned. "Lie down on the seat. No one must know where you have gone."

"Just get me out of here, Mol. They may not suspect that I am running, but take no chances. Get me away from here. Out of the clutches of the Coalition."

Molly MacMerkle, Donovan's legal secretary, nodded and hit the gas. As a Werebear, she had no allegiance to vampires. Even if questioned, she would lie with impunity. She was not controlled by the vampire code, and more importantly, she wasn't human. Vampires could sense when humans were lying, but Weres just confused them. "I know the ladies we're meeting. I have worked with them before — when Donovan had clients who needed to escape an abusive husband or pedophile father. They do good work. You both will be well-hidden and safe."

Molly gazed at Shirley, who was laid out across the back seat. "I hate that I'm going to miss the baby's birth. It would be so much fun watching my hot-stuff boss struggle with diapers." Molly sighed dramatically. "He deserves a ballsy little vampire who drives him nuts." She cackled. "He has had it far too easy for centuries. Time to shake things up a bit."

"If I survive, if the *baby* survives. We have no idea what's going to happen. This is new for everyone. Thank God Donovan has friends. Real friends who are prepared for anything." Shirley pursed her lips. "I am going to bear this child, come what may. And no Coalition of grumpy old men has the right to decide otherwise."

Molly's eyes gazed at her in the rearview mirror. "What *did* the Coalition decide? Why are you running?"

"Guilty for violation of the agreement and their paternity laws. Marilyn told me to run, and she wouldn't do that if I wasn't in danger. If my *child* wasn't in danger."

"Wow. Wretched ignorance at its best. I suspected they *were* gunning for you in the beginning. You and Judge Marilyn posed a mighty threat to their power. They were able to control her, but the two of you taking on the Coalition? You could not fail. And now they threaten the life of your child, possibly your life as well." Molly chuckled. "You already were a powerful woman. Now you're also vengeful. Pretty stupid on their part. Yes, you have to run."

Shirley nodded. A tear dripped from her eye. "Since I became a vampire, I have learned that they are a brutal culture. Everything is black and white. There is no room for gray. I wonder if they will ever wake up?"

Molly jerked the car and came to a stop. "I am betting on you and Marilyn." She pointed through her windshield. "Your next courier is in the car in front of me. Donovan will meet you at the second stop. Do not rest or relax until are you far away from here." She turned to Shirley. "Be safe, my friend. May the Moon Goddess guide and protect you." She pointed to the door with her head. "Now go. And welcome to the *jouhatsu express*."

Donovan ran up the steps of the small Lear jet and threw himself through the door.

A woman dressed in fatigues rushed over and shut the hatch. She pushed him into a seat and hollered, "Ok, George. Our last guest has arrived. Let's get moving."

The engine fired and the plane began to roll down the tarmac.

Donovan put on his seatbelt and looked around the plane. "My wife," he shouted. "Where's my wife?" His eyes rounded and he began to breathe heavily. Ye Gods! It was the second stop. This was where he and Shirley were supposed to meet. Once they were in the air, they would be safe.

It was difficult for vampires to fly in a contained aircraft. Once genetically related to bats, they had lost the ability to fly centuries ago. Fortunately, vampires had retained echolocation, the ability to detect the presence of objects — even in the dark — through the echoes that bounced off of those objects, whether it be breath, movement, machinery, or other sounds. Aircraft, however, rendered a cacophony of sound that rattled the brain and caused severe stress. When it was unceasing, it led to a form of madness.

Some vampires had embraced noise-deafening earphones or earplugs, while others avoided airplanes altogether. To move easily within the human world, Donovan had invested in an expensive pair of earplugs that shut out all extraneous noise. Thus, when they had prepared to flee, Donovan had insisted on aircraft travel. It made pursuit by other vampires difficult, if not impossible

The woman in fatigues shrugged. "I'm filling in for a member of the flight crew." She rubbed her ears and grimaced.

Donovan forced himself to hide his suspicion. By all appearances, she could be a vampire. She was obviously unaware of the effect of aircraft on her hearing. Was she friend or foe? Sure, a few vampires might volunteer for the underground railway, the *jouhatsu express,* but was that likely? On the other hand, the deep-seeded misogynism of the vampire nation would make it unlikely that a woman would be sent to detain him. Donovan took a few calming breaths, something he had learned in yoga. He would just have to keep a close watch and trust that the organization making them disappear was competent enough to keep them safe.

"Mr. Brennan?"

Donovan had been instructed to use a false name. It was a further safeguard against being found. No one knew his real name. Brennan seemed like a safe choice.

An older woman approached his seat. Also wearing fatigues, she was petite, with sharp green eyes and a finely lined face. Her closely cropped brown hair gave her the appearance of an elf. "I'm Nancy Phelps, your *jouhatsu* guide. As you know, our organization was contracted to help you and your wife disappear." The woman sat in the seat next to him and fastened her seatbelt

Donovan gazed at her. He tried to hide his panic "Yes, but I was supposed to meet my wife on this leg of our journey." The plane gained speed and lifted into the air.

Nancy smiled. "You wife was quite fatigued when she boarded. She is fast asleep in the bedroom in the back. After you have been briefed, I will take you to her. Given her delicate condition, I would prefer she be permitted to get some rest. We need her in top form so that we can get you to your destination."

Donovan sighed with relief. "I thought that . . . that she had missed the flight or that something had happened to the baby or that she had been detained . . ."

Nancy grinned and shook her head. "First-time fathers." She chuckled. "You're all alike. Nothing turns a man into a simpering wimp faster than a pregnant wife."

Donovan flushed. "I've already been the butt of numerous jokes. I just want to keep her safe, and this is the best I could come up with."

Nancy nodded. "Have you followed all of our instructions?"

"Yes, though I forgot about the phone until I discovered they were using it to track me"

Nancy's lips pursed. "Many forget. A phone is guaranteed to find someone who hopes to disappear. Have you closed all of your social media accounts"?

"Yes, but —"

"I advise you to stay off of the Internet from now on. It's tempting to go on there to check on family and friends, or to read stories about your own disappearance. However, every move you make can be tracked. Those trying to find you will be monitoring all of your accounts, as well as any searches containing your name. That is the second most common way people are found. Curiosity killed the cat, and in this case, it could kill you. You need to stay completely off the radar."

Donovan nodded. "My secretary will be issuing a statement that we are on an extended honeymoon and will not be available for at least a year. By then, I hope this matter is resolved. One way or another."

Nancy opened a large brown envelope she carried. "As long as no one knows your intended location, all should proceed smoothly, but keep a very low profile. You do not want to be recognized. I have all of your new identity papers here. Make sure you memorize them. I have no idea where you will be relocated. I don't want to know. But I have a general idea and have included some information on local medical practitioners and hospitals." She handed the envelope to Donovan. "These are my only copies. We have retained no others."

She handed him a ticket folder. "Our next stop will be

Frankfort. From there you will take a train to Prague and then a private flight to Brussels. A car will be waiting there to take you to your final destination. Wherever you wind up, please remember that although people may appear to be non-English speakers, they may understand enough to expose you."

Donovan studied the documents. He had long held funds in a Swiss Bank account under a false name, ensuring money would be available on short notice. He had a second account in the Cayman Islands. He had become skilled at relocating on a moment's notice, but this was the first time he had to disappear without a trace. Those hidden bank accounts would ensure he could afford to hide as long as possible.

No one in the human world would care that he and Shirley had disappeared. The Coalition, however, was in pursuit. Hopefully, the hopscotch path they were on would leave them stymied.

Nancy stood. "I will get you to the airport in Prague. From there, you will be in the hands of others. Since you have pre-arranged payment, there will be no further need for contact. Be cautious with any phones you use or purchase. They can be intercepted by satellites used by intelligence agencies, which means a motivated individual could find a way to track you." She patted his arm. "I'll let you know when your wife awakes."

Donovan turned, and out of the corner of his eye, he caught a flash of another set of fatigues. Was another crew member eavesdropping? Perhaps it was time to find out. Donovan snapped open his seatbelt and swiftly walked into the plane's kitchen. The woman who had greeted him when he boarded the plane was preparing something in the microwave. When the microwave beeped, she winced. As if her ears hurt.

Donovan rested against the doorway and studied her. Her obvious discomfort with plane noise made him extremely suspicious. If she was the enemy—another vampire—he needed to know before the plane landed in Frankfurt. He sniffed, then laser-focused on her face. No, not vampire, but he was sure she was not human. He cocked an eyebrow. "I didn't know Weres flew. I thought it messed with your receptor cells."

The woman glared at him, visibly startled. "Vampire," she hissed. "Do not toy with me. I am not here by choice." She gazed at him, her nervousness made apparent by her shaking hands. "Keep your voice down. I enjoy my job. I don't want to lose it."

Donovan cocked an eyebrow. "So, a Were then, but one with echolocation? Let's see, a whale, or a dolphin or a shrew, no . . . a hedgehog. Yes, most definitely a hedgehog." His eyes narrowed, but he held up his hands. "Don't worry. I have no wish to expose you, but you seemed unusually interested in me. You were snooping. I wish to disappear, not be exposed."

The Were shook her head. "I wasn't snooping. Every time Nancy rattled that envelope, it felt like someone was driving a large nail into my skull. I couldn't block it. So I merely peeked around the corner to check out the source.

"Why fly, then? If you knew the noise would affect you dramatically?"

"I had no choice. I'm a standby volunteer. Not on the first crew, but a fill-in for others. Usually, I'm a driver or site facilitator. This is the first time I was pulled onto a flight crew." She glared at him. "Don't worry, *vampire*. I won't expose you. I don't even know your name." The woman sniffed "You vampires are such an uppity bunch. It's always about you."

Donovan straightened and cast her a somewhat cruel smile. "As long as there is no further trouble, this time I'll give you a pass. But be forewarned. If anything unusual occurs on the rest of my journey that threatens my wife or child, I will react instinctively. You will be within my sights"

"Whattayagonnado, bat? Bite me?"

Donovan chuckled. "Not a chance. I'll merely shred you with my fangs and leave you for the wolves."

The Were paled and turned back to the microwave. She removed a mug of some steaming brew, blew on it, and took a sip. "Message delivered, vampire."

Nancy approached him. Her gaze darted between Donovan and the Were, and she raised her brow in question. "Is there a problem?"

Donovan shook his head. "None at all. Just passing the time." He moved away from the doorway. "Has my wife awakened?"

Nancy nodded. "Yes, and she's asking for you. Come, I'll take you to her."

The Frankfort Airport was a zoo. The echoes rolling off of the millions of objects in motion almost overpowered Donovan's earplugs.

Even Shirley winced, and her altered DNA had not yet enhanced her hearing. Still, she frowned. In perfect French, she said, "Wow, it is really loud in here. I swear I can hear a thousand different languages." They had been instructed to keep their conversation to a minimum, but when they did speak, they were to behave as if they were French citizens.

Nancy guided them through passport control and out of the airport. She hailed a taxi, which took them to a train station. Within an hour they were on their way to Prague.

The train arrived in Prague in the middle of the night. Nancy again hailed a cab, this time dropping them off at the Vaclav Havel Airport's private jet terminal. "You will be met at your plane by a young woman named Veronica. Her photo is in your materials. You may be approached by others within the terminal. Ask only for your plane and provide no further information. Because you are flying a private jet, your passports will be required only at the port of entry, in this case, Brussels. Do not offer your passport to anyone, and under no circumstances should you surrender it. It is the ticket to your new life."

Donovan nodded "Well, I guess this is where we part. Thank you for your assistance."

Nancy nodded her head and walked away. She was soon swallowed up by the travelers passing through the facility.

Shirley took Donovan's arm and yawned. "I am looking forward to a long nap on this flight. I need a good night's sleep."

Donovan peered at her wan face. He knew all of this travel had been hard on his wife, especially since she was carrying a child. He had noticed her drifting off on several occasions. While he wished he could have avoided their flight across Europe, they really had no choice. At least Shirley had passed her first trimester and was no longer experiencing morning sickness. That would have thrown quite the wrench into their journey.

Donovan gazed about the terminal, searching for the company providing their charter flight. In a discreet corner, he could barely make out the corporate logo he sought. Copeland Company, identified only by a black swish on a gold background. Elegant and refined. The company was wholly owned by the people who had handled his disappearance, making it less likely that they could be traced.

He guided Shirley to the check-in desk and pressed a key card against a reader. The machine beeped and the customer service agent checked her screen. She motioned to a door behind her. "Your plane is at Gate Four. Take this aerobridge to your plane. It leaves in exactly five minutes. Have a safe flight."

Donovan turned just as they passed through the doorway. The agent's screen was blank. She had already deleted their flight information. He followed Shirley down to the jetway, into a small plane.

A man dressed in combat fatigues awaited them. As soon as they entered the plane, he pulled the door closed. The man was tall and sturdy, his close-cropped platinum hair framing a rough-looking face. In heavily-accented French, he said, "Take your seats, please. We will be in the air in ten minutes. We will have immediate clearance." He walked away and went into the cockpit, taking a seat next to the pilot.

Donovan and Shirley sat in the front of the plane, as far away from the aircraft's engines as possible. Shirley smiled as he stuffed his earplugs in his ears. She yawned. "Glad I don't need those to sleep. I will be out like a light as soon as we take off."

Donovan smiled and patted her hand with affection. "It's a direct flight, so we will only be in the air for an hour and a half. We still have a long drive ahead of us. Brussels to Paris is about a four-hour jaunt, and it will be another two hours to our chateau near Les Andelys. So nap as much as you can. That's why I requested private cars with drivers. They will have room for you to stretch out and rest."

Shirley rubbed her stomach. "If our child allows it. He or she seems to be swimming away in here, and each day the movement becomes more and more pronounced." She yawned again. "Perhaps that's why I'm so tired." She rested her head on Donovan's shoulder.

Donovan smiled and kissed her brow. "I can't wait until we can remind our son of all the discomfort he caused you."

Shirley giggled. "And if it's a girl? Will you remind her as well?"

"Of course, my darling. That is a father's prerogative."

The plane's engines fired and it began taxing down the runway. As they lifted into the air, Donovan gazed at his wife. Her eyes were closed and her breath was even. Shirley had already drifted into sleep. He closed his eyes as well.

"Sir? We have some news."

Donovan's eyes flew open and he straightened his spine. His gaze fixed on the man who had greeted them. "What is it?"

"We received a message from our home office. We have been ordered to divert to Paris, sir. Apparently, there is a suspicious party awaiting your arrival in Brussels. She claims to be your sister."

Donovan raised his eyebrows. "My sister has no knowledge of my itinerary." And Marilyn would not make such an obvious move. "Yes, best we head straight to Paris then."

Shirley turned her head, but her eyes remained closed. "Except we were supposed to meet our guide for the rest of the journey in Brussels. What now?"

The man shrugged. "I will be driving you to your final destination. It would be too risky to wait for the other guide to travel to Paris." He offered a crooked smile. "We have to be flexible in this business. As it happens, your chateau is owned by my family. I can get you there quickly and safely." He stuck out his hand. "Name's Gerhard Durand."

Donovan shook his hand. "Andre DuBois, and this is my wife, Sophie."

Gerhard nodded and returned to the cockpit.

Shirley turned to Donovan, her eyes filled with concern. "Donovan, something's off. How did he know where we were headed? We never told him. His part of the mission was to end at Brussels. Wouldn't we be notified directly if our itinerary was changed? We have the burner phones." She shook her head. "What if it's a trap? Perhaps we would be better off . . ."

Donovan nuzzled her and whispered. "I am just as suspicious. When we land, we need to find a way to divert his attention and go off on our own."

"Where? Where can we go that's safe?"

"There is only one place we can go that no one will connect to us. Except for my sister, and she's on our side." He sighed. "We will be hiding in plain sight. But I am confident, it is the one place no one will think to look."

Shirley gazed at him. "And where is that?"

"A nunnery."

Shirley frowned. "A nunnery that welcomes vampires? How can that be?"

Donovan smiled. "They are turned women who chose to withdraw from the world, rather than face a life of bigotry and uncertainty. Women of God who live in defiance of their vampire legacy."

"Cloistered?"

"Yes, and living on an island that time forgot, quite literally."

Shirley frowned, "Shouldn't we be located near a large city where we can access healthcare? In case of —"

"They are self-contained, with their own health system. It is quite advanced and serves the entire island. My sister and I set up the trust that funds their operations."

"The island is populated with humans?"

"Yes, and the nuns serve them. They are an interdependent community. The humans are descendants of the original five families brought to the island. They run their farms, winery, fishery, and water purification and power plants."

"So the humans are blood slaves?"

Donovan laughed. "When first turned, the nuns chose to feed on animals or each other, rather than humans. To drink human blood would violate their religious beliefs. They were most mindful of passages in the Bible that forbade that particular practice. However, when turned, they appealed to the Pope for assistance. He refused to assist them. Whether out of ignorance or fear, or superstition, he proclaimed them *whores of the devil* and left them to flounder or survive. Back then, nuns were nothing more than servants, considered to have limited intellectual abilities. *These* nuns were expected to die out and quickly."

"But they survived?"

Donovan nodded his head. "Many of these women came from nobility. They were able to secure the funds necessary to fund their community. They were also better educated than most women of the time. They were well-trained in basic life skills, as well as math and sciences. Once they were cast out, they endeavored to learn any of the skills required for survival. My sister brought one of them into our law practice, and we helped her set up a viable infrastructure, one that was self-sustaining. Just because they were cloistered does not mean they weren't capable of adapting to their new world. Now, their health care and manufacturing processes are world-class." He tugged at Shirley's hair. "Given our situation, I regret that I did not think of them before. The convent is ideal for someone like you. Someone with a foot in both worlds. They have the expertise to deal with your pregnancy."

"The humans on the island accept that they are vampires, without question?"

"The islanders may suspect that they aren't human, but no one would dare question it. They live in Utopia, and they know it."

"Sounds ideal."

"Indeed."

When the plane landed at the Charles de Gaulle Airport, Donovan politely arranged to meet Gerhard outside the private charter terminal.

"My wife needs to be fed, and since we are headed into the countryside, it is best we pick up some necessities now."

Gerhard appeared displeased. "I am quite sure your needs have been properly anticipated at your chateau. If you need anything, we would be happy to secure it."

Donovan cocked an eyebrow. He wanted to challenge the man. After all, he had previously claimed the chateau belonged to his family. If that had been true, he would have been aware that the chateau had been sold a few weeks ago, to a private corporation registered in Switzerland.

His sister had made the purchase immediately after Shirley had been charged. Marilyn was a bit paranoid and insisted on preparing for every possible outcome. She had buried ownership in a morass of sub-corporations. Anyone intent on finding the true owner would have to drill down through six entities and then discover the title was held by Marilyn's doorman's deceased dog.

He doubted Gerhard even knew the name of the owners, much less its location. When they took the final step in their travels, he and Shirley had intended to abandon their sponsor and head to their new destination, several towns over. Getting into a car with Gerard could only end badly. And Donovan wasn't much in the mood for a deadly confrontation. Clearly, whomever Gerhard worked for did not have their best interests at heart. "Have you children, Gerhard?"

The man flushed. "No, I am not married."

Donovan forced a chuckle. "Then you have not had the glorious experience of pampering a woman with child. Not only are they eating for two . . .or three, they eat the strangest things. And they demand them at the most awkward times. In the past few months, I have witnessed the most unladylike behavior. I have no intention of encouraging it." He tapped Gerhard on the shoulder. "So, give me a few hours to prepare. We will meet you at the car when we are finished. I trust you will pick up the luggage?"

Gerhard's reluctance visibly eased. From his expression, he

believed that Donovan and Shirley would not flee without their luggage. "Of course, sir. You have the information on the car and where it is parked. I will wait for you there, with your bags."

Donovan hid his smirk. The man would be waiting a long time.

Donovan and Shirley walked leisurely through the terminal, arm in arm. They were the very picture of a happy couple on vacation. Occasionally, they slipped into a store, and made a purchase, then merrily moved on to the next.

When they reached the last business, they entered and grabbed colorful articles of clothing off of the racks. Donovan entered a dressing room and quickly changed out of his up-scale designer clothing into jeans and tee-shirt advertising some French rock band from another era. He left shopping bags filled with his original clothing in the dressing room and moved back out into the hallway. Moments later, Shirley emerged, dressed in similar clothing, but with a cap that hid her blonde hair. She had a much smaller purse wrapped around her waist.

A salesgirl appeared, and after stuffing a large number of Euros into her hand, Donovan quickly wiped her memory. Then he grabbed Shirley's hand and led her toward a door marked *sortir*. The exit took them to an alley populated with trucks and delivery people.

Donovan approached the first delivery vehicle. "Excuse me, sir, I wonder if we could get a ride to the main terminal?" He flashed a few Euros at the delivery man.

The man took the money and shrugged. "For that amount of money, I would drop you off on the Champs-Elysees. Jump in." He opened the side of the van and allowed them to enter, then closed the door and jumped up to his seat on the driver's side. "Where do you want to be dropped?"

"We're meeting someone at the taxi stand in Terminal Two E." Donovan smiled. "I haven't been back here for years. I wanted to show my wife a particular duty-free store in the private jet terminal, but now we're going to be late, and Henri gets grumpy when people are not on time."

Shirley giggled. "I am quite sure he will forgive you after you buy him a superior glass of Cognac."

The driver harrumphed. "There aren't many in this country who would refuse a good glass of that." He brought his van to a stop at Terminal Two E and pushed a button on his control panel to release the doors. "Here we are. Please close the doors tight when you exit."

"*Merci beaucoup,*" Shirley said, offering the man a sweet smile. "We greatly appreciate your assistance."

The man grunted. "I would never turn down money that goes into *my* pockets instead of my wife's."

Donovan helped Shirley out of the van and then studied their surroundings. "Let's head over to Terminal Two G. No sense in making it easy for anyone trying to track us." Just as they crossed into the new terminal, Donovan spotted a cab headed for the taxi stand. He flagged it down and they quickly settled in. "The Hotel Costes, please."

Shirley gazed at him. She leaned in and whispered, "Why a hotel? Shouldn't we be moving on?"

"We need a car. That place caters to celebrities. Discretion is their byword. It's the best place to be seen, but not seen. And a great spot to rent a car."

"Where are we headed?"

"The Port of Le Havre. I need to rent a yacht." He studied her. "I worry that this trip is putting too much stress on you. You haven't had a good chance to sleep since we left Chicago." His thumb gently swept the dark shadows under her eyes. "You appear exhausted."

"Once we board the yacht, how long will we be on the

water?"

Donovan glanced at the driver. It was hard to determine if he was listening. Carefully, he said, "Approximately eight hours, if the wind is blowing our way. Ten hours if it is not."

Shirley frowned at him, then catching his strange expression, waved him off. "Plenty of time for rest."

CHAPTER SIX: FORSAKEN

Shirley stood on the deck and watched the sun rise in the east. As the colors of the sky glowed red, orange, and yellow, she smiled. What a glorious start to a new day.

After arriving at Le Havre, Donovan had swiftly procured the services of a yacht that rented by the day or the week. He had provided the crew with the GPS coordinates where they would meet the representative of the nun's island to seek asylum, then boarded the ship. After they set sail, Shirley had immediately retired to the guest cabin and fallen into a deep sleep.

It was the scent of food that had awakened her. Her child seemed to be exceptionally hungry. *Always.* Shirley had no experience with pregnancy, so she had no clue if that was normal.

As she gazed at the ever-changing horizon, still munching on some sort of fried dough, Shirley sighed. So far, their voyage had been smooth, though the slight rolling of the yacht on the water occasionally made her stomach uneasy. Despite her minor motion sickness, she had slept soundly. Evading their captors had been exhausting. Now she felt rested and calm.

Donovan stepped up from their quarters and stood beside her, sipping on a cup of French Roast. "It's so peaceful out here. No sounds that offend or smells that repel. I don't even miss civilization."

Shirley made a face. "It's the smells that most concern me. My senses are not as fine-tuned as yours, but I already know our child detests tuna fish and peanut butter. A sniff of either makes my stomach turn."

Donovan placed his arm around her waist. "And what do you crave, my love? What would settle our child and make you smile?"

Shirley smiled. She took Donovan's hand in her own. "Safety. I want you, me, and our child to be safe. I want this nightmare to end. I want the Coalition to back off and stop threatening to steal our baby. Those men would stop at nothing to achieve their goals." She shivered. "They showed no sympathy for me or our child. They are the most horrible of monsters. I don't know how I can abide living among them."

Donovan hugged her. "I want you to know that my duty is to you and our child. Until the Coalition relents, I will keep you and little Harry safe. I will protect you until my last breath."

Shirley kissed his cheek. "Little Harry? What if it's Harriet?"

Donovan chuckled. "At this point, I simply don't care if it is boy or girl. We created this child. It's a gift. One to be treasured."

"I almost wish . . ." Shirley sighed. "But then we wouldn't be together. My turning was a condition of our marriage. It seemed like such a small sacrifice at the time, but now . . . now I question whether I can survive living in a society of misogynistic, narrow-minded assholes." She turned to Donovan. "I did it for love, only for love. I just hope our love is enough. Enough to withstand such bigotry . . . such irrational hatred. They subject humans to that which they fear most. Intolerance. They are guilty of that which they fear—surely they must realize that."

Donovan pulled Shirley against him and stroked her hair. "That is what Marilyn and I have been fighting for. To make them see. They believe it justifies their behavior. Many of those men have never entered the human world. They intentionally stay among their own kind. You and I know there is a different way, a better way. They think they are protecting the Vampire Kingdom, but in reality, they are dooming it. If we cannot find a way to safely reproduce, our numbers will continue to decline. More and more will choose to self-terminate."

Shirley held her stomach, sensing the slight movement of the child that grew within her. "Why can't they understand that we are bringing them hope? If I am able to bring this child to term — if I can survive the birth, then we have found a way to repopulate the Vampire Nation. To inject it with new blood. It may not be pure blood, but perhaps it is the correct evolutionary step. Obviously, something has made vampire women barren. That means something has to change. What if permitting a mating between a turned female and a vampire male has been the answer all along?"

Donovan nuzzled her neck and ran his hand down her back. "If we cannot evolve and adapt, we will die. One way or another, we will die."

A member of the crew approached. "Sir, the Captain has asked me to inform you that we are approaching the exact coordinates specified. What are your instructions?"

"When we reach that spot, aim the ship toward the west. Cast the anchor and send the message I provided over the channel specified. Then we wait. They will come to us."

Donovan led Shirley to the bow of the ship. He pointed to a metal bench. "Let's wait here, so they may see us."

"Wouldn't it have been easier to go to them? To bring this ship closer to the shore and motor in on a dinghy?"

Donovan chuckled. "Strangers are not welcome on this island. There is no beach, no real shore. No place to land a ship of any size. Over the years, the nuns have reinforced the surrounding waters with junk and sharp rocks, anything that would deter strangers. More than one ship has been left to sink, its sailors joining others on the ocean floor. No, we promised complete discretion. We cannot go to them. They must come to us. It is the only way to protect their location."

"Then how do we get there?"

"Very carefully." Donovan pointed to a small red ship that appeared on the horizon. "There is one ship permitted in and out, and without complete clearance, you are not even permitted to board," He smirked. "You might say they run a tight ship."

Shirley giggled. As the ship approached, she leaned against Donovan and smiled. "We're almost there. I can't believe we made it this far. Maybe now I can relax and enjoy my pregnancy." She peered up at Donovan. "Do you think we'll ever be able to return?"

"It is hard for me to believe the Coalition has taken things this far. Never did I suspect that they would react so harshly to our situation, but in the vampire world, compassion is not an acceptable response. My sister and I were lucky. Our long-time exposure to humans has taught us the value of compassion. Of all the qualities humans possess, their most admirable is their compassion for others. Their ability to support others in a time of need. I remember how people in America rallied after Nine-Eleven. They found strength in their compassion for others. It was demonstrated time and time again in their support of first responders, the victims and their families, and their country. You would never see a vampire abandon their lives and join the military to protect their nation after an attack. I am quite sure many vamps were puzzled by a nation that mourned such an egregious loss and then sacrificed themselves to prevent a reoccurrence."

He kissed Shirley on top of her head. "I am not an American, not in the traditional sense, but I was never more proud to be living among them."

"So, what will we do? Hide away on this desolate island

until we are no longer among the hunted?"

Donovan shook his head. "Right now, I have no answers. Except for one — no one will harm my family. If we are to live out our lives in exile, then we will do it safely, productively, and most importantly, will not fear to love, laugh, seize joy."

Shirley's eyes misted. "That's all anyone could hope for, be they human, vampire, or something in between." The red ship drew closer and it began to take shape as a fishing trawler. "What a strange flag on their mast. What does it mean?"

Donovan studied it. The colorful banner featured silver and gold keys crossed at the midpoint. A crown of roses rested in the center, a dove above flying off into the unknown. "The keys are taken from the papal flag. I believe they represent the power of *loosing and binding*, the heavenly authority given to believers in Christ. The crown of roses is a tribute to the Virgin Mary. That may be a reference to the order of nuns on the island. The dove is an expression of hope. It is the first time I have seen it, but I would guess the flag represents the beliefs the nuns and islanders hold."

The trawler threw anchor about one hundred feet from the yacht. A man dressed in loose trousers and a white tunic, his head wrapped in a colorful scarf, stepped onto the deck, his arms crossed across his compact body. His expression was almost defiant.

The captain of the yacht emerged from the control room. "Sir, they have requested that our representative approach. How do you wish to proceed?"

"I assume you have a dinghy?"

"Yes, sir."

"Have one of your men take me and my wife to the ship. We may be boarding, we may not. Either way, I imagine you would like your dinghy returned."

The captain frowned. "Are you sure you wish to subject

your wife to the open sea, given her delicate condition?"

Shirley placed her hand in Donovan's and offered a slight smile. "My husband has only my best interests at heart. No worries. I shall enjoy the journey." Softly, she said. "There is no way are you leaving me alone on this ship. Lord knows what he's up to."

Donovan forced a smile. "No, we shall go on together. We are hoping her sister will be on board."

The captain appeared puzzled. "But I thought . . . er, I mean . . . You said you were headed to the Azores. I thought this was to be a quick stop."

Donovan nodded. "To meet up with her sister. Just a little family business. We'll be back posthaste."

Though the captain did not appear convinced, he nodded. "You will have to proceed to the lower deck to board."

Donovan leaned into Shirley and whispered. "Why do I suspect someone is waiting for us in the Azores?"

They left the deck and walked downstairs to the lower deck and out a small door that led to a small platform, where a small dinghy awaited. Before they boarded, a ship's mate handed them life preservers. After those were fastened, Donovan and Shirley stepped into the dinghy and sat on a bench. The small watercraft slowly pulled away from the yacht and headed to the trawler.

When they pulled alongside the fishing boat, Donovan bowed and said in ancient Portuguese, "Two keys, one rose, the dove a shining light."

The man grunted and moved to lower a sturdy metal ladder over the side. He pointed to the ship's mate on the dinghy. "He stays behind?"

Donovan caught the ladder and nodded. He steadied it as Shirley climbed, then followed closely behind. In French, Donovan shouted to the ship's mate, "Return in one hour and we will be on our way."

The man nodded and spun the dinghy back toward the yacht.

Donovan turned to the trawler captain. "Pull up anchor and drift starboard to the yacht. I want to make it difficult for them to follow. They will lose too much time when they have to turn that bloody whale around."

Slowly the ship came around to the yacht's front. A lone member of the crew stood on the deck, his binoculars focused on the trawler.

Donovan guided Shirley to the shelter of the control room. "I caught just a glimpse of a weapon in that man's pocket. Bullets would not harm us, but they may harm our child. I am not taking any chance of that happening." Donovan stepped over to the very modern control panel. "What is the speed of this ship?"

"We can top out at eighty knots, sir. More if the wind is behind us. Do you anticipate a chase?"

"They may try to follow, but I doubt that yacht can exceed eight knots. They can try, but they are too big and bulky to succeed."

The captain smiled. "Then please, be seated and we will be on our way. We can play with them—head in the wrong direction until we are out of sight."

The island did indeed appear forbidding. In fact, it appeared uninhabited. The shoreline was treacherous, forbidden.

"Welcome to *Abandonada*, the island of the forsaken," Donovan murmured.

The trawler slowly passed through a series of locks that led to the inner island. When it pulled up to a dock, several women in white habits appeared. Their expressions were stern but tempered somewhat by their coifs—millinery masterpieces shaped like half-moons.

Donovan took a deep breath. "Ye Gods, nuns always make me jumpy. They are so intimidating."

Shirley giggled. "Ah, shades of Sister Prista Pruneface, my third-grade teacher. No ruler was too large or too small to convince the wayward child to adhere to the rules. But those hats. Wow. They are no doubt the envy of nuns around the world."

Donovan squelched a chuckle. "I must admit my association with nuns of any persuasion has been fleeting. I always feared the onslaught of holy water, though holy water is only a danger to witches, not vamps. Still, no one appreciates having water thrown in their face."

"Well, I suspect that is the least of our worries." Shirley examined the waiting congregation. "I know this order is quite secretive and secluded, but how do you know they will protect us? They may have no qualms about turning us over to the Coalition. They may fear that we will bring disruption to their island."

Donovan pondered her statement. Shirley was right. He had assumed he would be welcomed because he had assisted with the purchase of the island and created the trust that supported their order, but maybe that assumption was unreasonable. These nuns had made it clear they simply wanted to be left alone. Their ouster from the Church and subsequent exile had left them bitter. They had expressed no desire to associate with other vampires, in particular, the Vampire Coalition. Perhaps they *would* be unwelcome. "We are just going to have to hope for the best. Even if they shelter us for only a few weeks, it would get the Coalition off our trail."

The trawler docked, and a nun with a slash of red around her waist emerged from the crowd. After a plank was laid between the boat and the dock, she boarded the ship. She was tall but thin, her presence regal and commanding. The woman tilted her head as she gazed at them, her bright green eyes filled with curiosity. After a moment she smiled. In the same ancient Portuguese tongue Donovan had used with the captain of the trawler, she said, "Donovan Trait. You honor us with your presence. Why are you here?"

Shirley gasped and swayed slightly. Her face had gone white. Donovan gazed at her in alarm. Obviously, the past forty-eight hours had been too much. He swept Shirley up into his arms. He smiled at the nun. "Mother Superior, perhaps we can get my wife out of the heat first. She is four months along, and I fear our travels have put a strain on her. She needs to rest. After I get her settled, we can talk. I will tell you everything."

The nun nodded and turned, leading them off the boat. When they crossed to the dock, she turned back to the trawler captain and shouted, "Better get back into deep waters, Jorge. We have two more mouths to feed. We need more fish." She made a zipping gesture across her mouth. "And remember, if anyone makes an inquiry, *silenceo.*"

The trawler captain nodded, and the engines of the boat roared to life. With a soft *put-put,* the boat moved back toward the sea.

The nun gazed at Shirley and said in heavily-accented English, "My dear, I am Sister Rosalie, or Mother Superior to those who serve God in my order. I fear your husband's worry has made him lose his manners." She clucked he tongue. "He always was a bit impetuous."

Donovan groaned. "And you continue to treat me like an errant schoolboy. Allow me to rectify my sins. Mother Superior, Sister Rosalie, allow me to introduce my new wife, Shirley. She is newly turned. Chemically. And adjusting to life as a vampire. I fear it is not going well. Which is why we are here."

Sister Rosalie cast a weak smile. "Turning of any kind tortures the soul. Takes some getting used to." She led Donovan off the dock onto a path paved with stone. It wound around a wooded area and led to a large one-story building. "It has been almost a century since you last visited, Donovan. We have made significant improvements in that time. I trust your sister has shared our progress?"

Donovan nodded. "She has. Most impressive. A productive, modern society in a primitive setting."

Sister Rosalie walked into the building and took a sharp turn to the left, winding up at a door marked, *assistencia medica.* "With your permission, I would like one of our doctors at our health clinic to examine your wife to ensure she has suffered no ill effects from your travels. After she rests, of course." The clinic was set up like an American hospital. Medical personnel rushed to and fro. Islanders gathered in a waiting area, holding babies, tending to children, or just appearing ill. When they caught sight of Shirley and Donovan, all conversation ceased.

"Why are they staring?" Shirley gazed at Donovan. Her eyes filled with worry.

Sister Rosalie smiled. "We don't often have visitors. We have shut ourselves off from the real world intentionally. I am afraid you will be objects of curiosity throughout your stay. Do not be offended if the children try to touch your hair, Mrs. Trait. Blondes are an anomaly here, though some of our teenagers attempt to lighten their hair occasionally." She winced. "Which is preferable to the pinks, greens, and blues they experiment with."

Shirley nodded. "Not much different in our world. I would much prefer they touch my hair than my belly."

Sister Rosalie frowned. "That is unacceptable here. Curiosity is one thing. Unwelcome touching is not." She motioned to a man wearing a stethoscope around his neck. "Doctor Acosta is our lead physician here."

The man came forward, a bright smile crossing his brown

face. In stilted English, he inquired, "Welcome. How may I help you?" He extended his hand to Donovan.

Donovan set Shirley on her feet and shook the man's hand. "I am afraid my wife is worse for wear after our long journey. As you can see, she is with child. I imagine she is in need of fluids, food, and rest." Shirley leaned against him.

The doctor barked out an order, and a wheelchair appeared. "Off your feet, young lady." He nodded at Donovan. "We will take good care of her. Do you wish to accompany us?"

Sister Rosalie placed her hand on Donovan's arm. "Go with your wife, now. We can talk later."

CHAPTER SEVEN: TROUBLE IN PARADISE?

Donovan gazed at Shirley as she slept. He yawned. He could do with a nap as well. A pretty young nurse came in and checked Shirley's temperature and pulse. Donovan stood. "I need to find the Mother Superior. Can someone take me to her?"

"She is waiting for you in her office, Mr. Trait. Follow me." The nurse led him out of the hospital and into a courtyard. Donovan winced at the sun and pulled out his sunglasses.

The nurse gazed at him in surprise.

"Sorry, the sun is a lot brighter than the country I came from, I'm afraid. I will need some time to adapt." As Donovan surveyed the people moving around him, he realized that none of them were wearing eye gear. They seemed unaffected by the sun. How could that be? He would have to ask Sister Rosalie.

Donovan was led to a canopied patio, where the Mother Superior sat at a table, typing something into her computer. His brows arched in surprise. "So far, your replication of the amenities of the outside world has amazed me. And now Wi-Fi?"

Sister Rosalie closed her laptop and smiled. "We may be cut off from the world, but we have *not* cut out the world. Everyone has a computer and everyone has access to Wi-Fi. Many of our residents use it for long-distance learning. We also encourage them to explore other countries and other cultures. And occasionally, they choose to leave to visit those places." She gestured to a comfortable-looking chair and

Donovan sat.

He cocked an eyebrow. "You allow people to leave? I thought that was forbidden."

The Mother Superior chuckled. "When we first colonized this island, we wished to remain isolated. We had been rejected by Rome and shamed by other orders. In addition, our lives had gone from peaceful and contemplative to the horror of dealing with our forced turning. Although to us, suicide is a sin, many could not cope. Those first few years we lost half of our order to self-termination. We had been damned for no damnable reason. It threw us into a tailspin."

Donovan shifted uncomfortably. "That was after? After we set up the infrastructure for your continued existence?"

Sister Rosalie nodded. "Thankfully, your sister set up trade routes so that we could easily access what we required for survival and then further development."

"Marilyn says you have done well. That with all of the industries you have developed, you are self-sustaining and thriving. That is admirable and an incredible accomplishment."

Sister Rosalie shrugged off the praise. "It has been a struggle at times, but with the Grace of God, and a few changes to our vows, we have survived. Although the Church considers us an abomination and has rejected us, God loves all creatures, including vampires. We continue to be a faithful and committed Christian order. At first, we remained separate from the humans who populated this island, but after a time, curiosity on both our parts won out. Slowly, we merged into one finely-tuned society."

Donovan frowned. "Are they aware you are not human? That you are vampire?"

The nun smiled. "While our community consists of many simple, God-fearing humans, the lack of exposure to the outer world gives them no basis for questioning our continued and unchanged existence. I also suspect they suffer from a very common frailty. They cannot tell us apart. To them, all nuns look alike." She smirked. "I am sure to most, all nuns appear endlessly ancient."

Donovan returned her smile. "So, they are unaware that no one ages? No one dies?"

"I am sure we are a bit mysterious, but we are not evil. They have no reason to fear us. They may talk among themselves, but as I said, they have been isolated all of their lives. They do not know to question what they don't understand. All they see is the successful evolution of their island. Most have no desire to leave. But in response to your inquiry, those who wish to leave, may. Their return, however, is subject to strict protocol. Not all make it back. They understand that. They must weigh the risks."

"The risks?"

"Exposure to disease, an inability to re-assimilate, changes to personality, behavior, or attitudes that may threaten our security, and related issues." Sister Rosalie steepled her fingers, her expression one of sadness. "Unfortunately, many of those that leave are unprepared to enter modern society on the continents. Once they leave, we cannot protect them. A few have been jailed or exposed to other unseemly pursuits. Their innocence may be destroyed, and sometimes, that expedites their demise. So we don't discourage their departure, but we don't encourage it either. It is a gift to accept that sometimes, your best life is what you already have." She studied Donovan. "Now tell me why you seek refuge in *Abandonada*. What has happened?"

Donovan stared off into the distance, watching the palm trees around the nuns' compound dance gracefully. It felt like he and Shirley had been on the run forever, yet it had been less than two days. "The Coalition agreed to our marriage under rather strict rules. We granted them the right to monitor the conception of our first child. We wanted to help our scientists discover why vampire women are barren and whether a turned vampire can safely bear a vampire child. This was their first opportunity to determine what was possible with a chemically turned female. As you know, at some point, it was discovered that human women could not carry a vampire child to term. The baby developed fangs in utero and destroyed the amniotic sac, leading to miscarriage and the mother's death.

"Unfortunately, after we married in the human world, and despite our best efforts, Shirley conceived. We don't know when conception occurred or at what point in her turning, so our baby has been declared an abomination. Instead of seeing this as an opportunity, the Coalition convicted Shirley of violating the marital agreement."

Donovan closed his eyes and took a deep breath. "Shirley is most likely carrying a fetus that is part human, something that is forbidden and grounds for extreme measures. And since there has never been a case of a turned vampire pregnancy, there is a possibility that she may not have been turned sufficiently to survive carrying a vampire child. Then there's the whole problem of half-breeds. Is our child a vampire or only half? Our child is considered an abomination. A freak. And some want him or her dead."

The Mother Superior sighed. She shook her head. She stood and began to pace. At one point she stopped and began muttering. Finally, she gazed at Donovan. She pursed her lips and said, "Damn fools. This should have been an opportunity. Instead, they treat it like a crime. Their shortsightedness, the fact they cling to the old, rejecting the new, is why we never submitted to their governance. Vampire women are barren. They should be investigating every possible solution. From what you have told me, obviously, a bit of human DNA may make a difference." Her smile was tinged with sadness.

She returned to her chair and lowered herself slowly. Her expression became thoughtful. "You know, our physicians and researchers are some of the best in the world. Our neonatal care is superior to that offered in other parts of the world. We have a zero-mortality rate for live births and the occurrence of genetic anomalies or defects is quite low as well. Our isolation not only prevents the exposure of our existence but also protects islanders from the very things that corrupt their DNA. They have no obesity, diabetes, heart disease, and other common human ailments because they are not exposed to the causes of those conditions. Our community is not perfect, but it is exceptionally healthy.

"With your permission, we can do what the Coalition rejected. We can evaluate this pregnancy and pinpoint when conception occurred. We can determine at what point your wife was in the turning process when she conceived. We can also monitor your child's development and any troubling genetic changes. And we can intervene if the pregnancy takes a dangerous turn, for your wife or child."

Donovan studied Sister Rosalie. "But your researchers are human, are they not? Wouldn't disclosing our vampirism to them be a risk?"

"Not if we restrict access to those with whom we have shared our secret. At times, our altered DNA has provided a clue to the cause of certain genetic mutations. We have been able to discover the cause of many diseases, which has led to some creative solutions. Our researchers are thorough but discreet."

Donovan felt overwhelming relief. They had been right to flee to the nuns. "With my wife's permission, of course, we will cooperate. But what of our safety? Can you offer us refuge? Asylum?"

The Mother Superior smiled. "That was never in dispute. We are committed to protecting the young and innocent, in particular the unborn child. This is your refuge as long as it is needed." She extended a hand to Donovan. "Welcome."

Donovan grinned. He and his family were safe. On this tiny island in the middle of nowhere, they would have the opportunity to thrive.

It had been weeks since the Traits had arrived in Abandonada. Their days were leisurely, filled with the pleasures of a simple island life. The stress of their journey had lifted, but their worries remained.

Donovan gazed at Shirley as she frolicked in the convent pool with several children. In the middle of the Atlantic, there was no beach from which to swim. A freshwater pool was a safe alternative. Today, Shirley was teaching the children water safety, something she had learned as a teenage lifeguard in the human world. However, the children appeared more interested in her blonde hair and pregnant body than learning how to swim.

He chuckled as Shirley attempted to speak in their new language. Her words were often mispronounced or misspoken, but the children delighted in the attempt. When she got really confused, Shirley resorted to pointing or outlandish hand gestures. Somehow, she managed to get her points across.

"I just hope the children don't pick up my wife's Pidgin Portuguese." Much to the amusement of Sister Rosalie, Donovan had kept up a running commentary on Shirley's lessons.

The nun wagged a finger at Donovan. "Don't be so hard on your wife. She was thrown into the ocean without a lifejacket, yet she continues to stay afloat. Even though they don't understand each other, she and those children have found a way to communicate. And we really need her assistance. This island has too many watering holes, creeks, and waterfalls. We have lost children to drowning in the past. So, if they will not stay away, the least we can do is make sure they understand what to do when they get in trouble." She smiled. "Your wife is going to make a wonderful mother. Not everyone has that kind of patience with children."

Donovan smiled. He *was* lucky. He had found a companion for eternity, and Shirley's zest for life ensured that he would never be bored. His smile broadened. Children. Babies squalling, toddlers running, teenagers yelping. He had never allowed himself to picture life as a father. Now he could not stop the images from running through his mind. A loud noise pulled him from his daydreaming. It almost sounded like . . . Donovan shot to his feet. "Shirley! Get out of the water. We need to take cover. Now!"

Shirley pulled herself from the pool and hurried to her husband. "What is it"

Donovan pointed to the sky. "A helicopter, and it appears to be searching for something."

Sister Rosalie pulled them under a metal canopy, then urged the children to take shelter. "I don't know who they are, but they have made several passes over our island recently. We don't exist on any maps, so we are puzzled at how they found us. All they can see from the air is a thick jungle. This island should appear to be uninhabited. We have cloaked Abandonada with the finest of military technology, and any breech of our airspace within five hundred kilometers is met by our defense system." She shielded her eyes from the sun and peered up at the helicopter. "Scepter Industries. Does that sound familiar?"

Donovan shook his head. "As you know, most vampires don't fly. More likely it has something to do with Rome. Scepter would seem to indicate a symbol of royalty or sovereignty. More likely the Pope than the Coalition."

The Mother Superior snorted. "I assure you it has nothing to do with the Pope. When they exiled us, they destroyed all records. They have no idea where we went nor did they care. We were swept under the literal papal rug. Which leaves hunters sent by the Coalition or unknown insurgents. It doesn't really matter. We cannot be breached by air or sea. We have made sure of it."

Shirley pointed at the helicopter. "What happens when they try to parachute in?" The door to the hovering aircraft had opened. Someone with a helmet, goggles, and a parachute peeked out.

A look of horror crossed the nun's face. "Then they get caught in the electrified net that covers this island." She shivered. "We try not to activate it unless we're threatened. We have no need to harm wildlife. The birds. Climbing animals. Even flying insects. If it's activated, anyone or anything would be caught in fifty volts of pure hell." She made the sign of the cross and picked up the large rosary tied at her waist. She fell to her knees and began to pray in Latin.

The air crackled, and squawking birds flew out of the trees. Donovan peered at the person leaning out of the copter. They appeared to be ready to jump. "Don't do it. Don't do it." His muttering was almost incoherent.

The parachutist drew back into the plane, then leaned back out and dropped something. It hit the netting and immediately burst into flames. The burning object shot back up into the air and turned into ash. Caught in the wake of the helicopter, the ash flitted in the air, swirling like an unrepentant dervish. The door to the helicopter closed and the helicopter turned, heading away from the island.

Sister Rosalie rose to her feet and studied the sky, her relief apparent. A moment later, the electric crackle of the net stopped. The birds flew off into the sky. The air stilled, then the sounds of island life returned. The radio Sister Rosalie carried in a pocket within her habit beeped. "All clear. Thank heavens." Then she turned and beckoned to Donovan and

Shirley. "It's time to meet with our researchers. Come."

Shirley pulled on a robe and wrapped a towel around her head. A few weeks on the island had taught her that few formalities were observed. The nuns wore habits, but the rest of the islanders wore casual clothing typically found at tropical resorts. It was produced on the island and provided to residents for free. Donovan had been grateful for that. He and Shirley had arrived with only the clothing on their backs. Now their closets were full.

Donovan followed Sister Rosalie and Shirley back into the health center. They entered a small conference room, where two other nuns and two men in lab coats sat.

Sister Rosalie settled at the head of the table and gestured toward other open seats. "Please sit." She pointed at the nuns. "May I introduce you to Sisters Madelyn and Angeline? They are lead scientists in our neonatal unit." The nuns bowed their heads in welcome. "Seated across from them are two of our medical researchers, Dr. Maldives and Dr. Alvarez, who I believe you have met." The men stood and shook Donovan's hand. Sister Rosalie gazed at the group. "Shall we begin?"

Sister Madelyn stood and walked to a console set up in front of the room. She pushed a button and the wall converted into a whiteboard. A single DNA helix appeared. "This study was divided into two parts. The first was to determine the viability of the child carried by Mrs. Trait. To do that, we sequenced her DNA and examined it for the known genetic defects that could lead to miscarriage or defects in the fetus. We found none." Sister Madalyn pushed another key on the console and three DNA helixes appeared. "Fetal DNA can be detected in the maternal blood as early as seven weeks into the pregnancy. You are at sixteen weeks. Your ultrasound is not due for another two weeks, but I think we can safely say that during that test, you will learn that you are carrying twins. A boy and a girl."

Shirley squealed. "Oh, that's wonderful! Absolutely wonderful." She turned to Donovan, almost bouncing in her chair. "Isn't that wonderful?"

A stunned expression crossed Donovan's face. "I was prepared for one. Ye Gods! What am I going to do with two at the same time? It will be madness. They will be bloody demons. A single Trait is one thing, but two together?" He shook his head. "I'm not sure—"

Shirley kissed his cheek. "Relax, dear. There are two of us and two of them. We're bigger, stronger, and smarter. Surely we can handle them. And if we can't, we'll hire a nanny. But we will handle it . . . together." She smiled at Sister Madelyn. "I'm sorry for the interruption, but *twins*. That *is* incredible news."

Doctor Alvarez chuckled. "I'm happy you are so pleased. That makes my job easier." He nodded at Sister Madelyn. "Please, continue."

Sister Madelyn again pointed at the whiteboard. "The problem arises in their genetic composition. It appears your daughter is sixty percent human, forty percent vampire. Your son, on the other hand, is eighty percent vampire and twenty percent human." She paused and a concerned expression crossed her face. "We don't know if those percentages will change as they develop and as your body adjusts to your turning."

"Isn't that odd? I thought twins had identical DNA. How can their genetic makeup be so different?" Donovan's eyes narrowed. "What aren't you telling us?"

Dr. Alvarez cleared his throat and all eyes turned to him. "Fraternal twins share the same genotype, but different DNAs. That's why they look alike but are not identical. If they are fraternal, as we suspect, they will be contained within two different amniotic sacs. If they are identical, they usually share a single one. Our greatest problem at present is that we can find no studies, no documentation, of vampire pregnancies in humans. It is alleged that they sprout fangs, but we have no knowledge of timing or what in the DNA precipitates that. However, we do know that fetuses don't consciously know what they're doing in utero. They are acting on instinct. We suspect when they do grow fangs, it will be something new and they will try to figure out how to use them. Human babies in utero suck their thumb or toes. With fangs, a fetus *could* tear the amniotic sac and cause a miscarriage or premature birth, or injury to the mother."

"I am no longer human. The vampire physician said I was fully turned." Shirley turned to Donovan. "Right?"

Doctor Maldives set his clasped hands on the table. "You may be fully turned, but there is no way to determine whether your womb and your amniotic sac have sufficiently strengthened to withstand even one vampire baby's bites, and now two. We just won't know what will happen in utero until it happens. Especially when one baby is more human and the other is more vampire. Will both develop fangs? Will both attack your amniotic fluid sac? Or only the dominant one?"

Doctor Alvarez cleared his throat again. "There's a more important consideration. Twins are known to suck on each other's fingers and toes when in the same sac. How will that change with fangs? Are they likely to harm each other as well? We must be prepared to act quickly if something detrimental occurs."

Shirley's eyes misted. "This is too horrible to comprehend." She snuggled into Donovan. "This whole thing could be a nightmare."

Donovan rubbed her back in attempted comfort. His gaze swept the doctors and nuns. "What's your plan, then? You must have a plan. Ye Gods, this is my family. My wife and children. I can't lose them."

Sister Angeline tapped on the table and all eyes turned to

her. "Our plan is quite simple. Monitor the fetuses during their development. Act when the fangs form." She sighed. "We know human babies develop teeth and gums in utero, but the teeth are not forced out of the gums until after birth. We have no experience with vampire babies. There has never been one born on this island." She blushed. "As you know, nuns are celibate. So, we don't even know if the fangs are an anomaly that dissolve in utero or the babies are born with them. We have heard rumors, though, mostly by monitoring some vampire sites. We are quite literally running blind."

Donovan gazed at Sister Angeline. "Then what do we do?"

"If the babies are sufficiently developed, we can induce labor and tend to the babies outside the womb. We have an advanced preemie unit here. They will be well cared for." The nun ran her finger along the small laptop in front of her, squinting at something on the screen. "And if they are not sufficiently developed, we can remove them surgically and place them in an artificial womb, one they can't shred. We developed it just last year. It mimics the womb in every way." She shrugged. "It was initially developed for very premature infants or patients whose womb rejects a fetus."

Shirley's mouth dropped open. Then closed. "Wow, that's kind of amazing."

Sister Rosalie leaned forward, her expression earnest. "However, we will have to keep the twins together. Psychologically and physically. They will already be reliant on each other. If they are separated, the loss could be devastating. They might not survive. That means if one develops fangs and creates problems, you will have to decide how to proceed."

A single tear dripped down Shirley's cheek. She swiped at it. "I'm sorry, I'm a bit overwhelmed." She gazed at the Mother Superior. "I know the Vampire Coalition lacks your resources. If they find us and take us back, I will most certainly lose one or more of my babies."

Sister Rosalie cast her a sad smile. "Then we will just have to make sure they don't find you. I promise you, we will do everything we can to protect you and your children. For as long as you choose to stay. We are committed to sustaining life, not snuffing it out. Even as vampires."

Chapter Eight: A Deux

Shirley was silent as Donovan led her into their assigned villa.

The nuns had built sustainable homes for every resident on the island. Several villas had been empty upon their arrival, and they'd selected one with the view of the waterfall in the center of the island. Donovan didn't know when the Coalition would come for them, but he was sure they were coming. And when they did, he wanted to be sure he and Shirley were as far away from the point of entry as possible. Clearly, unless aided by an islander, the only possible way to access the island was by penetrating the treacherous coastline. If even an attempt was made, they would be notified, enabling them to escape to a safe house on the island. The nuns had considered every possible option to secure their safety.

Shirley settled onto a bamboo settee and sighed heavily. "I'm not sure I can survive the next few months. Between worrying about the Coalition, the health of our babies, and my possible death, how in the hell am I supposed to negotiate the stress? We should be going to prenatal classes to prepare for the birth of our children, decorating the nursery, sharing our journey with those who love us, talking to other parents of twins. Instead, we are forced to hide." A tear ran down her face and she swiped at it. "That isn't fair, Donovan. We should be rejoicing, instead, we are stressed and panicked. I can't sleep. I can't eat." She sobbed. "I may lose these babies before I can hold them in my arms. And even if they do survive, the Coalition may take that right away from me." She wailed. "I might never hold my own babies."

Donovan rushed to Shirley and scooped her onto his lap, settling into the settee with her. "Shush," he cooed. "Nothing will happen to you or the babies. I won't allow it. We are the best place we can be under the circumstances." He rocked her gently and rubbed her back. "We are safe. We have access to state-of-the-art healthcare. We want for nothing."

"Except our family." Shirley sniffled and burrowed into Donovan's chest. "Dammit. I want your mother. I want Marilyn. I want people who love me, who know me. People who are invested in my . . . our future. I know we're safe. I know we have great doctors and superior resources. But I was just settling in, getting to feel like I had a family. And that blasted Coalition ripped it away. It's not fair. It's not right." She pounded on Donovan's arm. "Dammit. How are you going to make it right?"

Donovan kissed Shirley's cheek, then her lips. Guilt consumed him. This was his fault. *All* his fault. He was the one who hid Shirley's pregnancy from the Coalition. He was the one who had banked on the Coalition welcoming the pregnancy, even though it had not occurred in accordance with their strictures. He had never imagined the depths of their intolerance. Their lust for cruelty. Their capacity for hate. He had put everyone at risk. Shirley. The babies. His parents. His sister. "We will find a way to end this, I promise you." He nuzzled Shirley's neck. "I will fix this or perish trying."

Shirley snickered and pulled away. She gazed at him. "Not much of a promise when it's almost impossible to kill you."

Donovan offered a slight smile. "That's not necessarily true. If something happened to you or our children, I would die of a broken heart. I don't need to go through the traditional ritual—separating the brain from the body and imprisoning the brain in embalming fluid so it can't reunite with my physical shell. No, a broken heart can do much more damage with less mess and less fuss."

Shirley shook her head and the tears flowed again. "No, no, no," she sobbed. "I won't be the reason you died." She threw herself again at him and kissed him passionately. Then she reached down and embraced his cock.

Donovan tried not to jerk away from his beloved. He had been warned about the mood swings of pregnant women. Dr. Alvarez had given him some literature on what to expect and some book that was purportedly the bible for humans during pregnancy. None of that had prepared him for the swing from despair to carnal desire. One minute Shirley was a weeping mess, the next she was throwing herself at him, initiating sex. These days he had begun to feel like his wife's sex slave. Was there a possibility his male appendage could become disjointed or otherwise damaged from overuse?

Yes, he had a healthy libido. He was full vampire, after all. But the demands to be bitten, to be roughly penetrated, repeatedly, and even anal sex, were overwhelming. Dr. Alvarez had assured him that sex would not harm the babies, but with the frequency at which it was occurring, there was a strong possibility that his children would be born with permanent dents in their heads.

Donovan stood, gently shifting Shirley in his arms. He kissed his wife deeply and walked them to their bedroom. Even he knew better than to make love to his wife on bamboo furniture. Ye Gods, if the settee collapsed and they were cast to the floor, he would have to spend the rest of the evening consoling his wife, assuring her that she was not fat.

Donovan gently laid Shirley on their oversized bed and crawled up her body. He pushed up her top and nipped at her swollen breast. His hand kneaded the other.

Shirley moaned, and her hand slipped into his trousers — the ones with a drawstring, worn by the men on the island — and stroked his cock. She gazed at him and smacked her lips.

"I love your cock. I want it inside me now." She tugged at his pants, then his shirt. "Off."

Donovan tried not to laugh. His wife's mood swings had been accompanied by a significant increase in bossiness. Sweet Shirley had assumed the personality of a Dominatrix. Donovan moved off the bed and complied, his swollen cock waving in salutation. When he reached to aid Shirley in undressing, she impatiently tore her cotton shift from her body and tossed it on the floor. Then she rolled onto her arms and legs and wagged her voluptuous backside.

Donovan grinned. Who would not want a bite of that? It had to be every man's dream—human and vampire. If they could survive it. Donovan's incisors lengthened. His arousal quickly peaked. With a joyous grin, he moved closer to his wife and took everything she offered.

Shirley shifted uncomfortably when the ultrasound technician rolled the greased probe over her stomach.

The man smirked. "I know, I know. It's cold. It can't be helped. If we warm up the probe, it isn't as effective. On the plus side, you get to see your babies. That's got to be worth the price of admission."

Shirley frowned. The technician sounded more like a mechanic from New Jersey than a resident of a remote island. Inwardly, she shrugged. The island has incredible internet and television access. Perhaps the man was a fan of one of the American shows featuring the Jersey shore. She turned to the screen as a loud echo was emitted from the machine.

"There he is, your son's heartbeat. Nice and strong." The man moved the probe around the perimeter of her stomach. "And there's his sister. She's a petite thing. She's lucky to be in a separate sac. Her brother is a bruiser."

"Is that unusual?" Donovan asked. "For the boy to be so

much larger than the girl?"

The technician shrugged. "Typically, boys weigh more and are longer, but it tends to depend on the parents. It's all genetics, inherited characteristics. If the father is slight, so are the boys. If the mother is petite, the girls follow suit. However, nothing seems off. They are both healthy and active. Your doctor will review these films and let you know if there are any problems. I certainly don't see any."

Donovan smiled and took Shirley's hand. "Well, then we will gratefully accept good news when we receive it."

"How many copies would you like?"

Donovan frowned at the technician. "Copies?"

"Of the sonogram. Pictures of the babies. To share with the grandparents and other relatives."

Shirley fought the sadness that consumed her. Her parents were dead. But Donovan's parents, Gwendolyn and Jonathan, and his sister, Marilyn, deserved to share in this. They could not contact them without revealing their location. Or could they? "Two copies for now, but would it be possible to have the photos put on a flash drive, so we could transmit them electronically?" Donovan again squeezed her hand, his expression filled with love. Yes, it was clear he missed his family, too. While he had focused on their new family, it would never be a substitute for those they had left behind.

"Certainly," the technician said. "We do that all the time." He placed a blue blanket over her belly. "I'll just go get the doctor. Then we can finish up." The technician left the room.

Shirley smiled up at Donovan. "Darling, I am sure it's hard not to have your parents here. Your mother would be so delighted about the twins. She's waited so long for grandchildren."

Donovan emitted a deep sigh. "My father as well, and Marilyn, well, she can be a pain in the arse, but I know she was looking forward to being an aunt. Vampires don't get much excitement in their lives — we tend to find comfort in a lack of change. But this . . . this miracle should be shared. It pains me that we cannot.

"My parents and my sister have been deprived of the reality and anticipation of our children's births. They can't watch them grow up. Ye Gods, will we ever be able to leave this island and rejoin them without fearing the Coalition?" He ran a hand through his thick black hair. "This is so wrong. We should not be forced to do this alone. Someday, the Coalition will receive their reckoning. They will be made to pay."

Shirley snorted. "That would require a coup. The women would have to rise up and conquer and throw the old coots out. That will not happen, as much as we wish it."

Donovan's eyes lit up. "Although, we might be able to rattle their cages, encourage a little dissonance. Maybe with the help of the sisters, we can agitate, raise questions, make members of the Vampire Nation see how they have been held back." His smile was filled with satisfaction. "Rebellion is repulsive to most vampires. But perhaps rebellion is our only choice."

Shirley studied her husband. He was a spectacular lawyer, skilled at strategy. He had waged mighty battles in the courtroom, sometimes seemingly hopeless ones. Yet, he had always emerged the victor, triumphant while his opponents wept. He had danced with the best of them — Clarence Darrow, Barbara Jordan, Thurgood Marshall, Ruth Bader Ginsburg, F. Lee Bailey, and so many others in Canada and the United Kingdom — and won. Was this his time to take on the Coalition, for David to take down Goliath? Did they have any other choice?

She gazed at her husband. "Yes, darling, it is time to rebel. It's the only option."

The kick almost knocked the book out of her hands.

"Alright, Alexander. Time to settle down and get some sleep. And stop kicking your sister. Poor Lilabeth must be exhausted. You wake her at all hours with all the tumbling going on in there."

Donovan put down the papers he was reading and chuckled. "I guess the technician was right. He is going to be a little bruiser. His sister will need to be a hellion just to keep him in line."

Shirley laughed. "Oh, that's a given. And it will be encouraged by his mother. No boy should be allowed to terrorize his sister. You certainly didn't get away with it."

Donovan smiled. "No, my mother would have bruised my bum with a wooden spoon. We had nannies, but my mother was the one who ruled the roost. While my father was buried in inventions and scientific discoveries with his friend, Ben Franklin, she was left behind to keep us in line. Back then, women did not have careers. Their children *were* their careers, and my mother was determined to raise a proper gentleman, a prince she could be proud of." He smirked. "Unfortunately, with her attention focused on me, Marilyn was the one who became the hellion. She terrorized all of my friends, even though she was younger. My word, we used to hide from her."

Shirley clapped her hands in delight. "I would love for my daughter to be a hellion. The one who leads the charge. I want her to know her worth and fight for her rightful place."

Donovan grinned. "No doubt a skill she will inherit from me."

"Or me. Or both of us. We have both been warriors in the courtroom, you as a lawyer, me as a judge. And your sister as a judge as well. This little girl has a lot to live up to."

Donovan held up his hand. "What if . . . what if she wants none of that and chooses to rest on her royal laurels instead? No university, no law school. Just shopping and lunching and high society galas instead? She may see no appeal in rebellion, she may instead choose to bask in her family's wealth and do nothing."

Shirley's eyes narrowed. "And what if your son is nothing more than a wastrel? A self-indulgent playboy who never works an honest day in his life?"

Donovan grinned. A low chuckle rose up from his throat. Then he emitted a belly laugh. "Well, if I manage to keep my arse out of jail after challenging the Coalition, I certainly will not permit my children to ride the flotilla of shame. After all, this fight is about them. For them. And for the future of the Vampire Nation. We will be telling them stories about how we took down those old farts and brought our world into this Century. Kicking and screaming."

Shirley studied him. "You sound awfully confident. Does that mean you have a plan?"

Donovan nodded. "I do. I plan to prove that current vampire law is asinine and until it is modernized, we cannot thrive. We cannot flourish. We will become extinct. We have the medical data, I have the legal precedents, and we have one great example of where we should and can be—humans."

Shirley giggled. "Oh, that will go over like a lead balloon. No one likes to be told they have failed to live up to their responsibilities, that they have held their nation back."

Donovan growled. "Ben Franklin once told my father that it is the first responsibility of every citizen to question authority."

Shirley snorted. "He also said we are all born ignorant but must work hard to remain stupid."

Donovan cocked a brow. "And he claimed to be a mortal enemy of arbitrary government, as am I. Our Coalition and their decision regarding your pregnancy and our children are arbitrary, and that is where I shall begin my argument. In fact, I shall open with a fitting statement from old Ben, *The Ancients tell us what is best; but we must learn of the moderns what is fittest.*

"Clinging to old beliefs has created stagnation. Ye Gods, there is not one pure-blood vampire younger than two centuries in our nation. Everyone else has been turned. And since the Coalition considers turned-vampires half-breeds, they have no power and no voice. We watch with arrogance as the human world grapples with issues of racism, sexism, and other forms of discrimination, but we are guilty of the same.

"I do not want my children to grow up in a world where they will be shunned, shamed, and excluded, their voices squelched."

"Donovan, if we had not met. If we had not produced children, would you feel the same? Or is it only the accident of my pregnancy that moves you to fight now? Because this belief in the need for change, this need to modernize the Vampire World, has to come from the very depths of your soul or others will see it as self-serving. Have you always felt this way or is this a case of situational tolerance because now you are personally impacted? That makes a difference."

"Shirley, do you really think so little of me? Look at the types of cases I have handled in the human world. I have had the privilege of serving the disadvantaged and the disenfranchised. My reputation in the human world is solid. There is nary a question as to where I stand on such issues. For centuries, I have fought for those who could not fight for themselves. My parents encouraged it and I embraced it."

Shirley smiled. "Then I will be proud to fight beside you. And I suspect your sister, father, and mother will as well. This is not a battle you should fight alone. It is a battle the Traits should fight as one." She arched her eyebrow. "My only regret is that no one turned Ben Franklin when they had the chance. He would have ripped the Coalition a new one. And it would be very much deserved."

CHAPTER NINE: WE ARE FAMILY!

"**Y**ou want to do *what*?" Donovan felt the sting of betrayal cloud his mind. And while he was beside himself. Shirley beamed at him, her expression one of sweetness and honey, though her words were not.

"The minute I caught wind of the Coalition's ill intent, your secretary, Molly MacMerkle, put me in touch with The Lynx so that he could create a way to communicate with your family if we were forced to flee. But only in emergencies. Basically, he created a link on an obscure website that appears to lead nowhere. He claimed it was untraceable, but could be used to signal a pending message in a drop box on the Dark Web. I think this was important enough to share."

Donovan honestly did not know whether be thrilled or angry at his wife. She'd had the foresight to set up a method of communicating with his family should things go awry, but in doing so, she might have put them at risk of exposure. He closed his eyes and attempted to calm himself. It was not a malicious act. In fact, it had been a brilliant one. Still, The Lynx—a Werelynx who worked as a private investigator as well as a computer wizard—could be bought. That cat was unapologetically greedy and not above accepting a little lucre in exchange for information. He might have already sold them out.

"He doesn't know where we are. How could he? When I sent the message, I used Sister Rosalie's computer. The island's Wi-Fi is cloaked so it can't be traced. There are no backdoors, and firewalls upon firewalls. When an email is sent from Abandonada, it bounces off a dozen satellites before reaching its destination. When mail arrives in the drop box, a notification is sent through the blind link. There are a dozen steps to follow before anyone can get into drop box. It requires a fingerprint, a retina scan, and a voiceprint. State-of-the-art security."

"And who has access?"

"Molly's boyfriend Joe has a grandmother who's a Were-lioness. Hates vampires. Says they stink. Won't get in the same room with them. But she adores Molly, so she agreed to be the middle-woman."

"I see. What happens when *she* gets the message?"

"She sends a notification via her burner phone to the burner phone held by the specified recipient. They receive a key code to a zip file that can be opened after following a similar security protocol. If they don't follow protocol, the key code gets them nothing.

Donovan sighed. "And what if after all that, the message falls into the wrong hands?"

Shirley giggled. "Doesn't matter. It's in code, a code that is used in one of those old teen detective stories. If you don't have the book or don't know of it, you'll never figure it out. It will be gibberish."

Donovan sank into an armchair. Again, he closed his eyes to contemplate. His wife *was* bloody brilliant. "Did you come up with that scheme alone?"

Shirley giggled. "Molly and Marilyn helped. Those two are positively diabolical. And watching Molly and The Lynx go at it was hilarious. He has the hots for her and she was not having it. Still, he didn't give up, at least not until Marilyn lit into him about sexual harassment. Then he sorts of slunk away."

"Why didn't I know any of this?"

"I felt it wise not to distract you while you were fighting

with the Coalition. Meanwhile, I was preparing to flee and that just seemed like a wise step. I *was* a Girl Scout. I prepared for every eventuality."

"Well, wife, I am filled with admiration at your preparedness."

Shirley smiled. She gave Donovan a power salute and yelled, "Team Trait!"

Donovan couldn't hide his amusement. If nothing else, his wife was going to bring his family much-needed energy. She had survived her turning with no obvious side effects. Now that her morning sickness had passed, she seemed to be sailing through her pregnancy, despite carrying twins. And she had adjusted to their exile with ease. Nothing seemed to daunt her. It was awe-inspiring. Shirley believed in fairness, freedom, and the rule of law, and she was willing to fight for each with her entire being. He might speak the words that would hopefully sway the Coalition and the Vampire Nation, but she was his inspiration.

Her years as a human had given her something his centuries as a vampire had not—a belief in the righteousness of man. Shirley wasn't naïve by any means, but she had little experience in the vampire world. Now she had been exposed to the ruthlessness, the cruelty, and the absurdly provincial attitude of his world. Although she would never voice it, no doubt she regretted her turning. Still, she was a warrior, willing to fight by his side because she believed in him. There was no greater love.

"Suddenly, I am instilled with unbreakable confidence, wife. We can do this."

"No darling, we *will* do this. Now, what are your plans?"

"I think our best chance is to appeal to the masses. As I see it, the Coalition majority has enforced archaic laws that have inhibited the evolution and growth of the Vampire Nation. Their unwillingness to change threatens our very survival.

First, there is the intolerance of what they call half-breeds. Then there is the refusal to recognize the competence of women and their right to have a seat or two on the Coalition. Then there is the reproduction issue. If we cannot procreate, our nation will eventually wither and die. We are losing so many to self-termination. The staleness of the vampire life provides no reason to carry on. The injection of new blood, so to speak, is necessary to thrive and grow. We reject half-breeds, give minimal rights to Weres who merge with vampires, and generally shut out the rest of the world. The fact is, we could learn from humans and Weres. Some members of the Coalition have a superiority complex and the result is suffocating stagnation."

Shirley tapped her chin, lost in thought. Then she sat up straight. "I've got it. A slogan to unite the masses. *Adapt or die.*"

"May I remind you that vampires do not die—not easily?" He smirked. "I much prefer a play on Ethan Allen's revolutionary war slogan, *Open up, you sons of vampire whores!*"

Shirley smiled. "I have the perfect opening to your final argument. *When in the course of vampire events, it becomes necessary for one to dissolve the political bands which have connected them to with another, we hold these truths to be self-evident. All vampires are created equal. They are endowed with unalienable rights, that among these are Life, Liberty, and the Pursuit of Happiness . . .*"

Donovan picked up her train of thought. "*That to secure these rights, government has been instituted among vampires, deriving their powers from the consent of the governed. That when a government becomes destructive of these ends, it is the right of vampires to alter or abolish it and institute new government, organizing its powers to affect their safety and happiness.* Yes, I was there when Americans declared their independence. I was awed by their certainty, their right to self-governance. They fought against the tyranny of the King, even though they risked their lives to do so."

Shirley grimaced. "Except we are engaging in a battle of words, not of men, I hope."

"Violence is not the vampire way. While there is a certain fear of bucking the Coalition, there is also a strong sense that life is passing us by. So many of us have transitioned into the human world. The opportunities are greater there. It is time to incorporate what works into our world.

"My father and I have tried, but the majority of the Coalition continually defeats us. I can't tell you what a battle it was to convince them to ban feeding on humans and transition to my father's chemical compound. They agreed only because the human world had surpassed us. They had made it more difficult for us to freely feed on humans. Cities grew, people began to settle next to each other rather than acres apart, and they developed an efficient system of communications. When people started to communicate better and compare notes, our activities got noticed. We could no longer hide."

Shirley shook her head and sighed. "You are so confident that they will listen."

"No darling, I am confident that I will *force* them to listen. It is time to get Marilyn involved. She has the support of vampire women. If she gets them riled up, the Coalition will begin to get nervous. And the nuns will help. We must develop a groundswell of support, so when I force the Coalition to a hearing, it is with the support of the masses. If we can manage it, I want every single member of the Vampire Nation watching. They have the right."

"It begins in the streets, so to speak?"

"Yes, these past few years we have watched the humans protest, seeking to force change. We can learn much from their strategies, but we do this peacefully.

"Have no doubt. It is time for the Coalition to be accountable to the vampires they serve. This is a revolution. Now, I need you to contact my sister . . ."

Judge Marilyn Trait Henderson turned the lock on the door to the all-gender bathroom in the Cook County offices of the State Appellate Court and sat on the toilet seat. She removed her burner phone, went to the appropriate site, and initiated the security protocol. The disappearance of her brother and his wife had brought her under the scrutiny of the Vampire Coalition. She knew she was being watched. She even knew that her phones were being monitored. But Marilyn was no dummy. She had made sure that she and the others would not be outsmarted.

While Marilyn wasn't a fan of The Lynx, that skanky cat knew his stuff. The communication network he had set up was far superior to anything the Vampire Nation had produced. Yet, Marilyn was the suspicious sort. A bathroom at the appellate court was one of the few places she could avoid surveillance.

She accessed the drop box and read the first message. "Some photos for you." A heart emoji followed. What was it with humans and emojis? It was like they had forgotten how to communicate in a common language. She opened the photos and gasped. Two embryos appeared. Twins? Shirley was having twins? Marilyn smiled, a rarity these days. She was going to be an aunt. Their favorite aunt, since Shirley had no siblings. This would be her revenge on a brother who had constantly ditched her when they were children. She would feed those babies sugar and rile them up and . . .

Marilyn frowned. *If* she ever saw Donovan again. She gasped. Would she ever see her niece or nephew? She didn't even know where Donovan and Shirley were. Her eyes misted. Damn the Coalition. It should never have gone this far. Her arguments had been sound, irrefutable really. Had she lost Shirley's case simply because she was a female, defending a turned human? That was the only explanation. The misogynist bastards. They were a bunch of racist chauvinists. Except for Donovan and her father, of course. They were more tolerant and willing to listen.

The rest of them were pigs, stuck in a time when females were property, not deserving of the right to own property or pursue a career, even vote. The only reason she was permitted to attend law school was because her father had intervened and convinced the Coalition it would be easier to concede and consent. Marilyn had a reputation as a troublemaker. The Coalition might consider her an annoyance, but she was gaining support from her community. Mostly female vamps, but some men. Her time would come.

Marilyn clicked on the second message. It was a quote from the American hero, Thomas Paine. *We have it in our power to begin the world over again.*

Marilyn squelched a squeal. She was overcome with an unfamiliar emotion—hope. Donovan and Shirley were sounding the call to arms. *Finally.* She could not suppress the grin that overtook her face. The Traits would fight all the wrongs inflicted on her and other female vamps. And probably the lack of tolerance shown to half breeds. Donovan and Shirley had a stake in this fight. Together, they would finally force change.

Carefully, she typed, "I await your instructions. Auntie M." Then she signed off, closed the burner phone, and slipped it into a pocket in her robes. The time had come for all right-thinking vampires to claim their due. She would no longer be silenced. Marilyn thrust her fist in the air. *Our time has finally come.*

Gwendolyn Trait went into her bedroom closet and shut the door. She moved to a wall with shelves that held her many shoes. She reached behind one of the boxes and pushed a button. The wall swung inward. She stepped through the opening and pushed another button so it would close behind her. Gwendolyn settled onto a plush overstuffed armchair and pulled the burner phone from her skirt. She paused, trying to remember the security protocol. *Retina scan, finger, voice.* Or was it *finger, voice, and retina scan*? Oh, dear. She hadn't really paid attention when that sleazy man had explained it to her. Perhaps she should contact Marilyn. No, that wouldn't work. She was to discuss it with no one. Damn these newfangled phones. She much preferred her Brittany Neophone. So much easier. And elegant.

"Okay, I can do this." Gwendolyn took a deep breath. She activated the phone and held the screen over her left eye. It beeped. Another screen appeared and she pressed her index finger against it. Nothing happened. Okay, maybe she was supposed to speak. She cleared her throat and said, "The quick brown fox jumped over the . . . brown hill." She repeated, "Yes, the brown hill." The screen remained blank. "Oh dear," she muttered. *Was it the brown dog? No, it was the quick brown fox jumped over the lazy dog. Yes, that was it.* She spoke again into the phone and it beeped. Another screen appeared and she pressed her index finger against it.

The phone beeped again and a message appeared. *Good morning, Gwendolyn Hastings Trait. You have a message.* Slowly, a photo formed. Gwen gasped as two babies in utero appeared. "Oh, my goodness, there are two. Shirley and Donovan are going to have twins. That's amazing." She burst into tears and began to wail. "I am never going to hold those precious babies in my arms. Oh, I hate that awful Coalition. They destroyed our family. I am never going to see my grandchildren." She swiped at her tears and stood, stiffening her spine. "Well, we'll just see about that. Dear Jonathan will be prohibited to join me in the bed-chamber until Donovan and

Shirley are back . . ." She choked back a sob. "With my amazing grandchildren."

She pushed a button and slipped back through the door. The Coalition had never faced the fury of the Trait women. She would take those ignorant bastards down!

Jonathan Trait heard the soft ping just as he was leaving his men's club. He had stopped by for a spot of tea and a friendly game of chess. He required a respite from all his worries—his family worries.

The flight of Donovan and Shirley has been unexpected and he was kicking himself, because in reality, it should have been expected. In fact, Jonathan believed it warranted. He had served on the Vampire Coalition for many centuries. His royal lineage granted him that right. But dammit, his fellow Coalition members were so entrenched in their ancient beliefs that their brains were petrified, mired in concrete. He and Donovan had been gentle in moving them forward, urging them to make small changes in pursuit of the larger goal—modernization of the vampire world. But it had been for naught. The Coalition had been ruthless when dealing with his son and daughter-in-law's predicament. Instead of embracing it as the opportunity it provided, they had reacted with hatred. Some had been positively venomous. He was so ashamed of the Coalition right now, he would very much like to resign. Unfortunately, without Donovan, he was the only voice of reason. He had to stay on the Coalition to control their rath.

Oh, how he missed his friend, Ben. That man had been a horny old devil. His sojourn to France in the late 1700s had proved that. However, his role in the birth of America would have been indispensable now. A revolution was coming. Jonathan could sense it. The Coalition would be blind not to recognize it.

The burner phone pinged again. Dammit. When Marilyn had given him the phone, she had winked and said it was for *family matters*. At the time, he had been puzzled. Now, he suspected it was his only link to his son, to Shirley, and possibly to his grandchild. The problem was, he didn't even know how to access the phone, or why it was beeping. All Marilyn had said was to use his *super brain* and follow the standard cybersecurity protocol. If he and Gwendolyn had been in Tenerife, that would have been easy. There, he had a safe room he used when secure communication was required.

Jonathan approached the building that housed the state appellate courts. Marilyn had once told him that the unisex bathrooms there was the only place she could clear her head and block out the world. Surely, the man on his tail would not follow him there, at least not into a public restroom with a locked door. There he could unlock the burner phone. The constant beeping had increased his anxiety tenfold. He could not help but worry that whatever message it contained concerned Donovan and Shirley. Vampires didn't pray. They were atheists by necessity, though sometimes, praying was a comfort. He sought that kind of solace now. Maybe prayer would help.

Jonathan ducked into the office building and rather than going through the security screening, ducked into the unisex bathroom available in the lobby. He smirked. He almost wished he owned a Superman costume. Emerging in full costume would no doubt baffle his watcher, though it might cause security to get involved. Jonathan locked the door, sat on the lid of the toilet, and removed the phone from his coat pocket. He swiftly moved through the security protocol and accessed the messages in his drop box. Upon opening the first, his face exploded with glee. Two babies. Not one, but two. If he had ever needed an incentive to take on the Coalition, this was it.

He tapped on the second message. *Give me liberty or give me death.* Yes! The game was afoot, as Holmes would have said. The Traits were going to take the Coalition down. Death wasn't an option for vampires, but there were worse punishments. A good old-fashioned shaming. Detention. Exile. As one of the few remaining pure-blooded vampires with royal lineage, Jonathan Trait wielded a mighty sword. It was time to remove that sword from its sheath. And protect his family.

Chapter Ten: Intruders

The war room, as Shirley had coined it, was filled with nuns rapidly typing as they stared at their computer screens.

Donovan could not help but be filled with pride. These nuns were social media mavens. They had accessed every vampire-populated internet discussion group, Facebook and Instagram page, and all other social media. The podcast led by Sister Rosalie, in which she challenged the Coalition and its inability to move into the new century, had also been genius. Using many of the tactics that humans used in political campaigns had reaped great rewards. The vampire world was abuzz. Vamps were starting to ask questions.

That was how a revolution was begun. Highlight the wrongs. Insert a few facts. Raise a few questions. Suggest that a situation could be bettered. Point the finger at those who blocked progress. Offer solutions. Pave a path for change.

The nuns had also been wronged. First, by the Pope, then the Vampire Coalition. They had fought back by building a better world, a free society that fostered tolerance through word and action. The outcome could have been vastly different after their convent had been attacked by a small army of rogue vampires, murdering some of the nuns, turning others. Yet, they had not permitted the evil that had touched them to destroy their hearts. The Pope might have cast them out, but they had remained committed to their mission — service to the less fortunate. Although they remained unknown, they had done much to improve conditions in the Third World.

"You seem lost in thought, darling. What's spinning through that brilliant mind?" Shirley gently pushed a wayward curl off of his forehead. "Having second thoughts?"

Donovan smiled. "I am just realizing how badly things have deteriorated among vampires. We thought ourselves superior to humans when we should have been learning from them. Ye Gods, we managed to create a practical solution to our lust for human blood, but we couldn't leave our ancient laws behind. It was so arrogant to assume that our society could remain the same, when so much around us had changed. Tyranny does not become us. We have always abided by the Coalition because it kept us safe from the human world and other paranormals. In reality, it was our fear the forced compliance. Without our leaders, we believed we would not survive."

Shirley studied her husband. "I admit, understanding your beliefs, your laws, has been difficult. We had Hitler, Mussolini, Stalin. You have the Coalition. There isn't much difference."

Donovan's mouth fell open. "If you felt that way, why did you agree to be turned? To join our world?"

"Because I met a vampire I couldn't live without. Sometimes, you have to make sacrifices to be with the one you love. I made mine. And until the Coalition turned on me, I never regretted it. I just can't understand how you and Jonathan tolerated it. How you could be one of them."

"My father had kept them in line for a century before forcing them to create a position for me. Together, we thought we could convince them to change."

"Ever hear the tale of the scorpion and the frog? The scorpion asks the frog if he can ride on his back to cross the river. The frog expresses fear that the scorpion will bite him during the crossing. The scorpion points out that then they would both drown. Thinking that's a worthy argument, the frog finally agrees. He permits the scorpion to crawl on his back and begins to swim across. Halfway there, the scorpion stings the frog. As the frog flails in the water, he asks the scorpion why he bit him knowing they both would drown. The scorpion says something like, *I couldn't help it. It's in my nature.* All of this time, you thought you were helping those scorpions across the river, but they bit you anyway, because that's simply what they do."

Donovan's eyebrows rose. "Are you calling me stupid?"

Shirley patted his cheek. "Of course not, dear, just too trusting. You and your father believed you had everything under control and discovered the hard way that you didn't."

Donovan grimaced. "I feel like I owe you an apology."

Shirley laughed. "Your sister and I would have pushed you until you reached the inevitable conclusion. It's time for reform. The Coalition has to go." She smirked. "So, man up, take charge and do what you were born to do. Right this wrong so my children and I don't have to spend the rest of our lives in hiding. None of us deserves that."

Shirley accessed the drop box and was pleased to find the documents requested. Marilyn had sent the entire volume of vampire law, a constitution of sorts. Shirley didn't possess the oratory skills of her husband, but she could research the hell out of the law, any law. And she could write circles around any argument. That was why she had been appointed a judge at such an early age.

Donovan had been living with vampire law most of his life. He had adapted and accepted. It would be too easy for him to overlook something. She offered fresh eyes, and possibly, a jaundiced heart. Shirley might no longer be human, but she respected the fairness and equity built into human common law. She and Marilyn planned to scrutinize the Vampire

Code, pick out ten of the most vulnerable laws, and propose effective solutions. However, they also planned to create the outline for a more modern code, one that eliminated all prejudice and intolerance.

Shirley settled into the most comfortable chair in their villa. Her babies were growing fast—her belly seemed to expand daily. The lack of knowledge about her type of pregnancy had everyone on pins and needles. No one knew when she would give birth, but at seven months, she was more than ready. How did women do this? She felt like she was hauling two whales in her belly. Soon she would need to place her stomach in a wheelbarrow just to walk around.

The sonograms had revealed that her son, Alexander, continued to grow by leaps and bounds, while Lilabeth lagged behind him. Shirley chuckled. The size of the package was no reflection of the greatness within. She barely topped five feet, but she had outperformed men of a much greater size. She was confident her daughter would possess the intellectual prowess she also possessed. Lilabeth might not be able to physically move mountains, but she would have the ability to slay dragons with her mind.

Shirley downloaded the ancient tome that controlled all vampires. Thankfully, it had been translated into English. Marilyn had assured her the translation was true, overseen by legal scholars in the vampire world. As with so many civilizations, vampire language had undergone a transformation that better suited the modern world.

Still, as she had learned, while one might assume a law that had fallen into disuse was dead and would not be enforced, the Vampire Coalition had proved those laws were merely sitting in a metaphoric vault, waiting to be reactivated at the Coalition's convenience. The code would require revision to ensure that this never happened again. Even if she and Donovan had not been caught in this legal quagmire, she and Marilyn would have found a way to create a document that was clear and fair.

Shirley shifted in her chair. The babies were active tonight, as if they could sense her excitement at the historic changes about to take place. As Donovan had said, they needed to deliver a *one-two punch*. It would begin with Donovan's eloquent delivery of the words that mattered, followed by the revision of the code in a language all vampires could embrace and understand. Shirley patted her stomach. "Soon, my little ones. Soon you will be born into a world worthy of your presence."

Alexander kicked, hard and true. Lilabeth rolled in her protective sac, her flutters a perfect accompaniment to her brother's show of force.

Shirley lay by the pool, her pregnant stomach pointed to the sky. She closed her eyes, content to wallow in the quiet. Soon, her days would be filled with two children competing for her attention, but for now, she intended to enjoy the peace and quiet of Abandonada.

"There you are. I've been searching everywhere for you." Donovan settled into the lounger beside her. "Where are all the children? Usually, the pool is overflowing."

Shirley yawned. "They went fishing with some of the nuns. Apparently there is a magic cove filled with hungry fish, somewhere on this island. This really is an idyllic place for a child to grow up."

"And it may be where our children grow up as well. We could do worse." He took Shirley's hand and kissed her fingertips. "In fact, this would be a wonderful place for all of our children, if we are so blessed."

Shirley chuckled. "Talk to me after these two get out of diapers. Who knows? Maybe we can create a few more. Wouldn't that annoy the Coalition?"

"Not that we would fill our home with children merely to

annoy the Coalition." Donovan's head jerked toward the horizon. "Oh, no. It looks like our friends are back. We had better take cover."

The whine of the net activating filled the air. Donovan and Shirley moved under the eaves off of the pool.

A helicopter appeared and hovered over the island. Scepter Industries was once again painted on its side. "Same company. I wonder who they are."

Shirley pointed. "Look. I think they're going to attempt to jump."

The door to the copter slid open and someone in an orange jumpsuit peeked out. The person turned and went back into the aircraft, then returned holding a small black box. He or she tossed it toward the island. The box seemed to tumble in the trees, then came to a stop against the security net. Sparks flew and the net sizzled, but the box remained intact.

"The box must be made of metal." Donovan gazed at the tree where the box had landed. "I wonder what's in it."

"We shall soon find out." Sister Rosalie appeared beside him. "One of the security crew will grab it once the helicopter leaves."

They watched as it hovered. Then the airman shrugged and closed the door. The copter made a wide sweep of the island and flew away.

Sister Rosalie beckoned to Shirley and Donovan. "Let's take this inside. I will want your guidance after I view the contents of that box." She led them to her patio. "It will be a moment before security retrieves and scans the box." She poured them each a glass of iced tea. "Perhaps we will finally learn the mission of Scepter Industries. They have become pests."

A security man rushed in with an envelope. "The box contained a tracker. So we disposed of it and removed its contents." He handed her a white business-size envelope. "We also scanned the envelope. It appears to be clean."

The Mother Superior nodded. "Thank you. You may go." Using a letter opener, she slit the top of the envelope and removed a sheet of paper. Something else fluttered onto her desk. She quickly scanned the letter, then picked up the other piece of paper. "Reparations. From Rome. Someone has sold us out." She handed the papers to Donovan.

He examined them and shook his head. "Ten million Euros. Almost an insult for what they did." He read the letter and his eyebrows rose, then handed it to Shirley.

Shirley examined both and frowned. "It's a trap. If you cash the check, then they know you are here. If you respond, they know you are in receipt and they have the right location. Once they have that location, what will they do? Take over the island? Expose it? Destroy it? There is no way the Vatican will reveal its past behavior. They want to cover it up, and the best way to do that is to eliminate the evidence. You and your sisters." She paused. "I know the new Pope is much more liberal than past pontiffs, but can he be trusted?"

Sister Rosalie's eyes narrowed. She lit a match and burnt the letter and check. "I hope this is the end of it." She sighed. "Sadly, I shall have to conduct an investigation into how Rome found us, especially when we did not wish to be found."

Chapter Eleven: Staggered Arrival

Shirley awoke. Panic filled her. *Oh, no. The babies.* She rolled over and grabbed Donovan's arm. "Darling? I think we need to get to the Health Center. Something is most definitely wrong."

Donovan's eyes opened slowly. Then he sat up and his ice-blue eyes gazed at his wife. "What?"

"I think I may be in labor. Something is leaking, and I don't think it's me. I think my water broke."

"But the doctor said . . ."

"I don't give a damn what the doctor said," Shirley snapped. "I'm telling you something is wrong and you need to get me to the hospital, *now.*"

Moving slowly as if not quite awake, Donovan kicked his legs off of the bed. "I suppose I should call for help, then. There is no way you can walk to the center in your condition." He stumbled over some clothing that had been left on the floor. "I should call . . ."

"Yes, darling, pick up your phone and call. *Now.*"

Donovan reached for pants, no doubt to cover his naked-ness.

"Donovan," Shirley said firmly. "Phone first, then pants."

"Okay, okay. Give me a chance to think. In all my centuries, I have never done this before. I need to think. I—"

Shirley glared at Donovan. When had he become such a blathering fool? "Donovan. Give me the phone. We don't have time to think." She grabbed the phone out of his hands and quickly punched in the code they had been given. When the call was picked up, Shirley said, "Hello, I am in need of transport to the health center. I think my water broke . . . or something. Anyway, I need assistance with transport. I don't think it's safe to walk." She listened to the response and then disconnected the phone. "They're coming." Her hand swept her naked body. "Now, help me get dressed. I don't want to send the medical staff into shock."

Donovan zipped up his pants. He grabbed a Mumu Shirley had taken to wearing and tossed it to her. "Quickly, now. We must hurry."

Shirley rolled her eyes. *Really?* "Thank you, darling." She struggled to pull the garment over her head. "Panties? I can't go to the hospital without panties."

"Ye Gods, woman. The babies are coming and all you can think about is panties?" Donovan ran to a dresser and began to paw through the drawers. Finally, he found a pair of underwear and tossed it to Shirley. Then he sat on the edge of the bed and ran a hand through his bed hair.

Shirley struggled with the panties, and when she stood, more fluid ran down her legs. The babies weren't due for two months. Until now, there had been no evidence of fangs. Perhaps those had finally emerged. Whatever the problem, she was used to Donovan being calm and deliberate in a crisis. Now, he was behaving almost . . . like a human. Shirley was not sure she liked that. She adjusted her clothing. A knock sounded at the front door and she began moving toward it. "Put a shirt on, please. I don't want the nurses ogling what belongs to me."

Donovan pulled a tee-shirt over his head and raced over to Shirley. He scooped her up in his arms. "Let's go, my love. I've got you."

Shirley felt a stabbing pain and winced. "Just get me to the gurney."

Donovan got to the door and looked between it and

Shirley. An expression of panic crossed his face. "I need to put you down to open the door."

"It's open," Shirley yelled.

Two men rushed inside with a gurney. Donovan laid Shirley on top of it and the men rushed back out the door, with the gurney. "Wait a minute, I'm the father." Donovan threw up his hands and followed. "Oh, I don't suppose that matters. I am nothing but the sperm donor." He raced after Shirley. Suddenly, he yelled, "Ye Gods! I'm going to be a daddy!" He fist-pumped and puffed out his chest. "Pandemonium, here I come!"

Dr. Mendes spoke to Donovan with a solemn voice. "I'm afraid there is a problem, and it's one we did not anticipate."

Donovan took a deep breath. "My wife. Is my wife okay?"

Doctor Mendes nodded. "Mrs. Trait is fine, given the circumstances."

"Then what is the problem?"

"The problem is Alexander is ready to be born. He has moved into the birth canal and his amniotic sac has broken. Lilabeth, on the other hand, is content to remain in the womb. She is quite petite and would benefit from a few more weeks in gestation. Her sac is intact."

"But it's been barely seven months. Can either of them survive?"

"The problem is, we don't know anything about vampire gestation. Our experience is only with humans. The term of pregnancy with a vampire may be accelerated. We just don't know. It would be helpful to consult a female vampire who has given birth, but that's not possible. Yet, they both appear to be fully developed. I suspect both can survive outside the womb, and if not, we are fully prepared to deal with any complications."

"What do you recommend?"

"Let Alexander proceed. Allow Lilabeth to follow when she is ready. We could induce birth, but it's best if it occurs naturally."

"Then they won't be twins, just siblings?"

"They developed in the womb at the same time, so they are considered twins—with different birth dates. In unusual circumstances, twins can be born days, even weeks apart. However, once Lilabeth realizes her brother has left the womb, she may speed things up and follow."

Donovan nodded. "And what does my wife say?"

"She wants nature to take its course, even if she has to go through labor twice, weeks apart."

"Just look at him. He looks just like me." Donovan chuckled. "Look at that head of hair." He held the swaddled baby to his chest and kissed the black curls that peeked out from under a blue cap. He unwrapped the blanket and began to count the baby's toes. "And look, he has all his digits. Ten fingers and ten toes. Amazing."

Alexander mewled and kicked out his legs. Donovan quickly rewrapped the blanket around the infant.

Shirley giggled. "As both humans and vampires do. Now give me my son for a moment." Donovan placed the baby in her arms and she gazed at Alexander with adoration. She nuzzled him and smiled. Then she handed the baby back to Donovan. "Lilabeth appears to be making her move. She may have been slow to join the party, but she is determined to catch up."

Donovan settled into a chair in the corner of the room. A nurse appeared in front of him and held out her hands. Donovan snarled. "It's okay. I can hold my son. I won't drop him."

The nurse grinned. "Just a safety measure, Mr. Trait. Once the next birth begins, you will need to focus on your wife. I'm just moving him to the bassinet." She pointed to an institutional clear plastic bassinet set up in the corner. "Then Alexander can witness the birth of his sister as well. Once Lilabeth is examined by the doctor, she will join her brother. It will settle both of them. Reintroduce them to the familiar. We have found that twins do not react well to being separated."

Shirley moaned loudly and sat up. "Oh Lord, it's starting all over again." She glared at Donovan. "Why couldn't *you* give birth to one of them? It's the least you could do after knocking me up."

Donovan stared at her. What the heck had happened to his sweet, calm wife? She had grown quite angry with him during Alexander's birth. He wasn't sure how to handle it. Vampires did not show emotion, but Shirley most certainly did. Maybe a chemical turning failed to tweak that particular gene. Donovan kissed his son on the forehead and handed him to the nurse. "Obviously, I am needed elsewhere."

He stood and walked to his wife, then took Shirley's hand and tried to school his features into an expression of calm. "Just breathe, darling. Remember, breathe through the pain." Which was another problem. Most vampires were immune to pain. Yet Shirley had emitted bloodcurdling screams throughout Alexander's birth. He did not have any knowledge of the biology of turned vampires, but obviously, Shirley could experience pain. That was something left to be investigated by qualified professionals.

Shirley scowled. "I need drugs. Good, solid, hardcore drugs. Get them, *now*. Or get the hell out of my room. You are no help to me." She began to yell. "Just get out!"

Alexander wailed and Donovan's attention was diverted to his son. Ye Gods. Even his son was upset by his wife's behavior.

A nurse rushed to her side and began to repeat the breathing exercises. "I am so sorry, Mrs. Trait. As discussed, we cannot administer any anesthesia because we cannot know how it will impact the birthing process of a . . . a . . . non-human." She flushed. "I am so sorry."

Shirley burst into tears. "Oh, I am such a horrible mother. My son must think I'm a witch. I made him cry." Tears ran down her face. She began to sniffle. Then she clutched the corner of the sheet covering her and began to dab at her face. The nurse handed her a box of Kleenex. She grabbed it and set it aside. Just as Shirley prepared to use the sheet as a handkerchief, the nurse pulled a tissue from the box and forced it into her hand.

Donovan hid his frown. How was he to aid his wife when one moment she was crying and the next chastising him? Finally Donovan took a deep breath and sat down on the bed next to Shirley. He pulled her into his embrace and crooned, "It's all right, darling. I know you're exhausted. I am sorry it is you who must do all the work." He kissed the top of her head. "If I could do it for you, I would. I promise you I would." He kissed her lips. "But Lilabeth needs you now, so she can join her brother. We need to be strong, so we can welcome her properly into the world."

Shirley sniffled and blew her nose again. "I'm sorry. I know I'm being such a baby, but Donovan—I'm exhausted. And I hurt. I *really* hurt." Her face screwed up into a pout. "You promised me it wouldn't hurt, but dammit, it feels like I gave birth to a horse or a car."

The nurse turned away to hide the slight smile on her face.

Donovan knew if he erupted in laughter, he risked permanent impairment.

"I don't know if I can do it again." Shirley moaned and buried her head into his chest. She continued to sob.

Donovan gazed at the nurse and raised an eyebrow. He made a face that clearly communicated his feelings of helplessness. *What do I do now? What if she refuses to deliver Lilabeth? What if when the doctor asks her to push, she refuses?*

Shirley emitted a soft hiccup and gazed up at Donovan. Her face was still wet from the tears, but the flow had stopped. She smiled. "I'm so sorry. I feel nasty. I must *look* nasty. I want to take a shower and sleep for days."

Donovan smiled and gently stroked her sweat-laden hair. "To me, you are the most beautiful woman in the world. Even more beautiful as you birth our children. What a gift you have given me. First, your love, and now, two children. I am in your debt, and it is a debt I can only repay with love."

Shirley seemed to perk up. She stiffened her spine and smiled at Donovan. "I guess that goes both ways." She took a deep breath. "Let's get this done."

Donovan gazed at his wife, a baby suckling at each breast. The expression of pure happiness on his wife's face was worth everything they had gone through. He chuckled as the babies locked hands. The bond of twins was obviously strong, and these two were most definitely bonding.

Dr. Mendez entered the room and smiled at the scene before him. "Not only are they bonding to their mother, but they are also bonding with each other. How strange it must be to be floating in the womb, knowing there was another being beside you, yet being unable to touch it." He laughed. "You will soon find that those two already know each other well. We are convinced that babies can communicate with each other in the womb, even if they don't share the same sac. That will continue throughout their lives. Trust me, at times their ability to communicate without words will freak you out. Parents of twins always complain about it. They feel left out. My suggestion is, don't fight it. Let them form that bond. They need it."

Donovan watched his much larger son clutch Lilabeth's hand. "I imagine my daughter is going to have to learn to suffer the protectiveness of her older brother. Already he is reaching out, ensuring that she is safe."

"Well, she may be smaller physically, but she may catch up. Or be quicker, or more intelligent, or more motivated to succeed. Unlike identical twins, fraternal twins only share about fifty percent of their DNA. Throw in the vampire factor, and there is no way to know how things will play out. They are siblings, twins by accident of birth, but they may grow up to be very different beings."

Donovan nodded. He had examined each child carefully, amazed at their physical differences. Both of his children possessed clear blue eyes, but he had been told that could change. Only Alexander had been born with thick black hair. Lilabeth's head was covered with tufts of light brown. He wondered if Shirley had birthed *mini-mes,* one of Shirley and one of him.

Lilabeth fell back from Shirley's breast, drowsy. Her tiny rosebud mouth formed into a yawn. Alexander, however, appeared to be suckling without restraint. When Lilabeth's hand dropped from his, he stopped nursing and stared at his sister. He almost looked concerned. Upon viewing his sister in slumber, he returned to Shirley's breast. Alexander's hand again reached for Lilabeth's, touching this time, not grasping. Allowing his sister to sleep.

Donovan walked to Shirley's side and gently lifted Lilabeth. He cradled the child, holding her to his chest. He settled into a rocking chair and watched her sleep. She was a miracle. One the Coalition had threatened to destroy. Under his watch, they would never come to harm. He turned to Dr. Mendez and softly asked, "When will we know their genetic characteristics?"

"We'll let them settle overnight and run the tests in the morning. We should have answers in a day or two. But this is the time for bonding. With each other and their parents." He gazed at Donovan and smiled. "See how peacefully she sleeps in your arms. She senses she is safe, surrounded by love."

Donovan kissed Lilabeth's downy head. "Why did neither develop fangs?"

Dr. Mendez shook his head. "That's a mystery to me. We were able to see them develop in their gums, but like human teeth, theirs never sprouted. There is so much we don't know. Not only are we dealing with the merged DNA of a vampire and human, but we are also dealing with the altered DNA of a human in the process of being turned. We sort of know the what's, but we don't yet know the how's or the why's. That's going to take some time. Our researchers are thorough and to the impatient may appear to work slowly, but when they deliver the results, you can be sure they are correct. We will get the answers you need."

Lilabeth stirred and Donovan began to rock to calm her. With a small sigh, his daughter settled back into sleep.

Dr. Mendez smiled at the baby girl. "You know we have been working with incomplete and unverified information. For example, we have no reports of human females actually dying while pregnant with half-vampire fetuses. We know that female vampires are barren, but could the belief that female humans cannot safely carry a half-vampire fetus be a myth? Or disinformation?"

Donovan stared at the doctor. "Why would anyone—"

"To prevent vampire males from propagating with human females? To prevent the birth of half-breeds? There could be all sorts of reasons. My point is it could be *a big lie*. An attempt to maintain the purity of the vampire species."

Donovan's eyes flared. That would mean the Coalition's anger was not about violating the marital agreement, but about the possible discovery that they had lied. They might have been protecting themselves.

"Ye Gods. That's diabolical."

CHAPTER TWELVE: THE GREAT LIE

The Lynx paced the floor of the library in Judge Marilyn Trait's home, pondering his latest assignment. For a vampire, this chick was a looker. He wouldn't mind hooking up with her, taming those fangs, elevating her temperature a few degrees. Oh, the trouble he could get into under her robes.

"Cat, pay attention. And stop looking at me as if you want to take a bite. Seriously, my bite is far worse than yours." Marilyn's eyes narrowed and her blood-red lips curved up into a cruel smile. "I have had *real men* for dinner. Why would I waste my time with a Were?" She waved a hand in dismissal. "Stop behaving like a horny teenager and let's get down to business."

The Lynx paused and stroked his mustache. Sweet Goddess, he loved a woman with fire. He had been devastated when he discovered that his one true love, the Werebear, Molly MacMerkle, had pledged her troth to a Werelion. Perhaps he could woo this luscious vamp into his bed chamber and feast on her ample curves. He smiled seductively at the judge. "At your service, Your Honor. Please, whisper sweet nothings in my ear. Bring me to my knees with your exotic essence. I am at your command. I shall crawl through the driest desert, march through the thickest forest, plunge into a rushing river. All in pursuit of your desires."

"Oh, cut the crap, cat. Molly told me you trolled in bullshit. I should have worn my boots. Now pay attention. My brother Donovan needs your help, and his secretary, Molly, says you are the best. I need a private investigator, one who isn't afraid of getting his hands dirty, and I am pressed for time." She glared at The Lynx. "Sit. I can't stand an animal that prowls."

The Lynx sat and flicked away non-existent lint on his finely tailored suit. "I am not an animal, I'm a Were. A human with the ability to transform into a lynx." He gazed at her. "I have all the equipment necessary to turn you into a begging, screaming, weeping female whose only thought is how quickly I can make you scream. And after I have wreaked every possible orgasm from that luscious body, you *will* come back for more." He meowed.

Marilyn snorted. "Or in a moment of passion, I will shred you with my fangs and feed you to the rats."

The Lynx stared at Marilyn in horror. "Threatening my very existence is not an effective way to secure my services, Your Honor. Perhaps I should be on the first train out of here. The Metra, that is. I wouldn't want to get stuck on the *Bitch Express.*" He leaped off the chair and landed lightly on his feet. "Funny, I thought Donovan's sister would have a little more class. Now that wife of his, Judge Shirley, she's a real lady. Elegant, gracious, kind. A pleasure to work with. You, on the other hand—"

"This *is* for Shirley and Donovan." Marilyn tugged at her mahogany hair. "I am sorry that I am behaving like a raging bitch. Ye Gods, I despise females like that. It's just that Donovan and Shirley are in real trouble, and I'm trying to help, but I'm stuck. I don't have the skills to dig deeper."

The Lynx turned to her, assessing her. He pulled at a tuft of hair protruding from his ear. "How on earth could that lovely woman ever find herself in trouble? She's an angel. One of the finest humans I know."

"Except she is no longer a human. She has been turned. And while she was in the process of turning, she fell pregnant. In violation of the marital agreement she and Donovan made with the Coalition. The Coalition decided to put Shirley under house arrest and take possession of the children when they were born—"

The Lynx cocked a fluffy eyebrow. "Children? As in more than one?"

Marilyn took a deep breath and nodded. Then she spurted, "If she survives the pregnancy—because everyone knows that vamps should not get humans pregnant. Vampire babies grow fangs in utero and shred the womb, killing the human female. The Coalition said Shirley's womb wasn't strong enough to carry vampire babies and she would probably die. In this case, the fangs never developed and they were born just fine. Now, Donovan thinks the thing about vampire fetuses growing fangs was all a big lie to discourage mating between vamps and humans, and he is furious. He wants to know who started that lie and why." She stopped and took another deep breath. "I was able to trace the claim back to the eighteen hundreds, but I don't know who made it. Donovan thinks it was a member of the Coalition, and if it was, he wants to string him up. In the alternative, he wants to start a revolution and toss the members of the Coalition out. Except vampires don't know how to do revolution—"

The Lynx held up a hand. "Lady, slow your roll. Now, start from the beginning."

Marilyn glared at him. She pursed her lips, and her ice-blue eyes narrowed. She harrumphed, her disgust made plain. "I need you to find out who started the rumor in the eighteen hundreds. About the inability of female humans to carry vampire babies because their wombs would supposedly be shredded by the fetuses' fangs, leading to death. Apparently, vampire fetuses don't grow fangs. They develop them long after birth, not in utero. I can give you the names of the suspects. They are all current or past members of the Coalition. All of them also supported a law that banned half-breeds from the Vampire Nation. Denied them all rights granted vampires."

Marilyn grimaced.

The Lynx cocked his head. "You also consider turned humans half-breeds. Something we Weres have always found ludicrous. Vampires were created from humans. In the early days, most *were* turned-humans. Pure-blood vampires born of two vampire parents were rare, but even then, they would have still possessed some human genes. Vampires came from humans. Period."

Marilyn's eyes flared. "Don't lecture me, cat. I am well aware of the hypocrisy behind our laws and traditions."

The Lynx smirked. "Perhaps the genetic mutations that occurred affected your long-term memory. So easy to forget what you don't want to remember."

Marilyn tapped a blood-red fingernail on the arm of her chair. She reached for a flash drive that rested on a side table and clasped it in her hand. "All of the information is on here. You will be paid a fee of two million dollars."

"Is this a computer job, or one that requires actual interviews of vampires? Because bloodsuckers make me twitchy. I know there's a treaty and all, but I've heard stories." He shook his head. "I'm not sure it's worth it. The risk—"

"Three million," Marilyn snarled. "And you'll have help. From a few vampire nuns. They will go where you send them. Conduct any interviews. You forget that our sense of smell is acute." Marilyn sniffed the air and made a face. "Your smell is quite offensive. Like a wet dog. You would have a difficult time getting a vamp to speak with you. Nuns, on the other hand, will be received with respect and civility. You train the nuns, supervise them, and collect the information we need."

The Lynx shrugged. "Even Weres don't mess with nuns. But that in no way protects me. Four million, and you've got a deal."

Donovan's head was swimming. The Coalition's betrayal, the rabid hatred that perpetrated the lie, simply astounded him. He and his father had not even suspected they had been deceived. They had been sold a bill of goods. They were just as gullible as every other vamp.

The motive behind the big lie was to control vampires. To prevent them from introducing half-breeds into the Vampire Nation. An attempt to keep their blood pure. Donovan snorted. Ye Gods, vampires used to drink human blood. That blood didn't sicken or kill them. It had kept them alive. Nourished them. Humans had provided their lifeblood. Why had he never seen that?

Vampires had fomented a culture of hatred, of fear of humans. Initially, that logic was sound. Humans had hunted, mutilated, tortured, and killed them. There had been a reason to be afraid, to remain cautious. Humans destroyed what they did not understand. But so did vampires.

Unfortunately, at the forefront of Donovan's worries was the fact that Shirley had been forced to turn vampire, when it might not have been required at all. She had been condemned to eternal life without reason. That was unforgivable. Would she ever forgive him? He could not blame Shirley if she ended their marriage, took their children, and returned to the human world. He deserved her scorn, her derision, her hate. When he had revealed his suspicions, Shirley had merely frowned. She had made no accusations, expressed no anger. But perhaps once she recovered from the shock, that would come.

Donovan heard one of his children cry and he ran to the nursery. The health center had rushed to set it up, with all sorts of monitoring equipment. No one knew what to expect with his children. They didn't even know what they didn't know. All they could do was watch and respond.

Donovan smiled at his son. The baby was red-faced as he bellowed about his parent's latest offense. He swept the little bruiser into his arms and laid him on the changing table. He knew Alexander had been fed an hour ago. There was no way the child was hungry again. The fumes wafting from his son's diaper, however, indicated the true cause of Alexander's discontent. Quickly, Donovan cleaned up the mess and replaced the diaper, careful to stand off to the side to avoid projectiles of any kind. When he finished, he held Alexander up to eye level. "When you grow into a teenager and find me a bore, I hope you remember that I changed your nasty nappies." He chuckled and nuzzled Alexander's belly button. Then he carefully rewrapped his son's blanket around him and laid the swaddled baby next to his still sleeping sister.

Donovan felt a hand rest gently on his shoulder and he turned. "Shirley, you should be sleeping, love. You must be exhausted."

Shirley sighed. "Every time one of them cries, I wake up. Then I lie there, worrying something is wrong. I am exhausted, but I can't sleep for more than an hour. Then I lie there worrying about us."

Donovan frowned. "Us? Why on Earth would you be worried about us?"

Shirley took his hand and led him out of the nursery. She walked to their bedroom and crawled back under the covers. After arranging some pillows behind her back, she took Donovan's hand again and gazed into his eyes. "We need to take care of the elephant in the room, darling, I don't blame you for what's happened. We were both duped. My word, the entire Vampire Nation has been duped. You need to know that I would have undergone the turning process, even if I hadn't been warned that conception of a half-vampire baby might kill me. I wanted a life with you. You could not be turned human, so it simply made sense for me to turn vampire."

Donovan shook his head. He tried to curb his rage. The first time he'd heard about human deaths from vampire pregnancies was in the late eighteen hundreds, a time of significant change in his world. Vampires had emerged from their self-imposed isolation. They began to associate with humans, rather than hunt them, mostly by necessity. He had been among the vampires who actually preferred the company of humans.

At the time, humans were swept up in a whirlwind of social change. Humans had evolved and adapted so readily it had made him dizzy. As more and more information emerged about infertility among female vamps, even he had begun to seek the company of more pliant human females. Not because they were fertile, but because they lacked the bitterness some female vamps now associated with sexual congress.

And when the stories about human females dying from vampire pregnancies began to emerge, he had been horrified. Even though human females had pursued him in great numbers, when Donovan did take advantage of what was offered, he had always been careful to take the steps necessary to prevent pregnancy. In no way did he want to be responsible for the death of another, even a human.

He had accepted those stories as truth. Ye Gods, they had been repeated often enough. And when a lie was told often enough, people stopped questioning it. It became fact. What had been the purpose? To avoid the birth of half-breeds? To prevent the integration of humans, even turned humans, into their world? That spoke of targeted and unyielding intolerance. Hate. Even in his darkest days, Donovan had never felt hatred toward humans. But he was guilty of believing in the superiority of vampires over humans. He had believed his own species was genetically and morally superior.

Donovan no longer knew what was the truth and what was a lie. The very foundation upon which the vampire world was built had begun to crumble.

"For the life of me, Shirley, I cannot understand why I

believed the lie. Why I accepted it without question. I did not personally know of any human female who died because they were carrying a half-vampire fetus. In fact, I was skeptical when I first heard it. Who does the lie benefit? We are a species frozen in time because we could no longer propagate. When humans cannot reproduce, they find other options. In-vitro fertilization, surrogacy, synthetic wombs, adoption. We did not explore those options because it involved merging with humans. Our stagnation is our own damn fault."

Shirley frowned. "At first, I thought the Coalition wanted to monitor my pregnancy so they could find answers to vampire infertility. Now, I know that's not the case. Someone on that Coalition wanted to make sure the truth remained buried. They could not afford to allow my pregnancy to continue because it would expose the truth. That's why they were so punitive. The question is, who was the instigator? Who needed to protect their ass and why? Donovan, find the man or men who benefited most from preventing the birth of our children, and you will find those behind the great lie." Fury filled her eyes. "Maybe it was fear that gave birth to the lie. But hatred is the fuel that drives it.

"My fear, darling, is that the Vampire Nation may not survive this. You want a revolution, Donovan. This revelation could lead to the apocalypse. The end of the Vampire Nation. I know you're angry, but you must tread carefully."

Chapter Thirteen: Confrontation

Donovan approached the nondescript building where the Vampire Coalition was meeting in secret. His father had not been invited, nor had he. That in itself was a violation of the Vampire Code.

However, all Donovan required was a chance to speak to the entire Coalition in one place — the opportunity to speak his piece. Expose the lie. Humiliate the liars. Provide a path for redemption.

Donovan smiled at his father. "You go in first. They'll be shocked at your presence."

His father chortled. "I do wonder who will be the first to expose their fangs." He pulled out a small canister of pepper spray. "I don't need fangs to protect myself. One whiff of this stuff, and their senses will be overwhelmed. In fact, I might spray it even if they don't attack. They deserve it."

Donovan smirked. "I imagine their attention will quickly be diverted when I appear. When they come after me, you have my permission to unleash your weapon."

"Are the women in place?"

Donovan nodded. "And the babies. I only hope they can keep Alexander and Lilabeth quiet. The element of surprise is vital."

Jonathan stopped before a set of closed doors and turned to his son. "I will go in and take my seat. Join us in one minute." He opened the door and slipped inside.

Donovan heard shouts and angry words, mostly from those they had identified as the guilty parties. He waited for a moment, then walked toward the doors and flung them open. "Good evening, you bloody arses." Donovan leaned against the doorway, his smirk plain. "Meeting without me or my father?" He clucked his tongue. "So unprofessional, and a clear violation of the Vampire Code. Oh my, oh my. What shall I do?" He tapped a finger against his lips as if contemplating, and shook his head. Then Donovan pushed away from the door and entered the conference room. He strode to the table where the Coalition sat, placed his briefcase down, and proceeded to remove a laptop computer and a flash drive.

Harold Hannigan's dark brown eyes narrowed with rage. His fangs emerged from his gums. Some spittle dripped from his lips, not unlike venom from a serpent's mouth.

Charles Bengotten sniffed as if Donovan's essence was repugnant, and his mouth curled up into a cruel smile. He was clearly fighting to restrain himself. "How dare you show yourself after everything you have done. The list of charges is long and growing. We have a dungeon with your name on it." He sneered. "And where is your wife? A fugitive from justice. I sincerely hope her day of reckoning is upon us."

Hannigan grunted. "Did you expect anything different from a half-breed?"

Donovan ignored them. Instead, he closely observed the other members of the Coalition.

An expression of alarm crossed Mortimer March's face. His already pale complexion turned gray. His eyes filled with fear. After a moment, he murmured, "Oh, dear." Then he looked away and focused on an obscure painting on the wall.

Alexander Holmes' reading glasses slipped down his nose. He had to struggle to keep them on his face. Finally, he gave up and threw them onto the conference table. "Summon the guards," he snapped. "This man is guilty of aiding and abetting a convicted criminal. He should be in chains."

Ah, suddenly the gentle, unassuming scientist had grown

a backbone. Donovan hid a chuckle. Or perhaps the mad scientist routine was an act designed to cover up more nefarious behavior, such as hiding a vindictive mind and vengeful heart.

Donovan remained calm. "You might want to wait on that, old boy, considering that who should be in chains is a matter of dispute. I am quite sure you do not want the information I possess released to the rest of the Vampire Nation, the very vampires you are sworn to serve and protect." He grinned. "They are already in an uproar over your leadership. What I have here will be the match that lights the flame." He cocked his head. "Hell, I could revive the old mantra, *burn, baby, burn.*"

Bengotten's face reddened. "Enough," he roared. "Say your piece so we may end this farce and deal with you appropriately. You are guilty of treason and should be eradicated from this Earth."

Jonathan Trait stood. He glared at Bengotten. "You have always been an arrogant twit. However, I suggest you hold that acid tongue until you know the truth." Jonathan paused and a sly smile crossed his face. "Unless, of course, you already know it."

Bengotten opened his mouth, a retort clearly in the making. Then he stopped and ran a hand through his styled light brown hair. "You're insane. We have ruled this nation for over two hundred years. Without incident."

Donovan studied Bengotten. He shrugged. "All that proves is that the conspirators among us are consummate liars. They have crafted a tale that no one would question because there *was no reason* for us to question it. What began as a lie was told often enough that it became part of the fabric of our nation and once lodged there, no one felt the need to disprove it."

Donovan's eyes settled on Hannigan. "Tell me, Harold,

what motivated you to spin such an evil tale? One that tore hope from the hearts of our women and destroyed our very ability to thrive and evolve? What sort of heart lurks in that morning coat? In my mind, a dead one. One so shriveled from disuse that it has hardened into a wad of gristle. Barely beating."

Hannigan shook his fist at Donovan. "Call the guards, I say. I should not be forced to entertain such blasphemy. Such slander."

Donovan grinned. "Ah, but isn't the truth an absolute defense against slander? Well, Harold, I *have* the truth."

Holmes leaned forward in his chair. "Then speak, Trait. Give us your truth so that we may end this, you." He nodded at a man sitting quietly in the corner. "Roger, I suggest that we tape this vulgar display of disrespect. We may need to stream it to the nation in defense of the lies he has been spreading."

Bengotten's face reddened. "I don't think—"

"Silence," Jonathan Trait bellowed. "Let my son speak. Then you may prosecute him as you wish."

March nodded. "Yes, let the man speak. I am intrigued by his words. Please, Lord Trait, tell us about this alleged lie."

Donovan turned on his laptop. He studied the screen for a moment, then began to speak. "Throughout history, we have watched with arrogance as the human race engaged in conflict after conflict caused by disinformation, sometimes outright lies.

"In seventeen eighty-eight, Sweden's King Gustav the Seventh dressed royal troops in Russian military uniforms and ordered them to raid a Swedish outpost near the Russian border. You see, the King was about to be ousted by the masses. He needed a little distraction. The attack launched a two-year war that unified the people and kept King Gustav in power.

"In eighteen seventy, Prussia's Otto Von Bismarck tricked

Napoleon the third into declaring war against the better militarized Prussia. He released a false communique that described a polite meeting between Kaiser Wilhelm and a French envoy as volatile and fraught with conflict. Napoleon was so incensed that he declared war and France was soon in the hands of the Prussians.

"The Spanish-American War was caused by a lie about the bombing of the USS Maine. Hitler launched a world war on a lie. Even American involvement in the Vietnam War was spurred by a lie.

"Lies become rumors and, after many repetitions, are accepted as truth. We are not discerning information gatherers. We tend to ignore the noise around us unless and until we are directly impacted. I am guilty of this. We all are." Donovan began to stroll along the length of the table as he spoke. Then he stopped in front of Hannigan and continued.

"A member of this very Coalition craftily spun his own lie. In eighteen sixty-nine, he started a rumor that humans could not survive impregnation by a vampire—that the mother's womb would be shredded by the fangs of the fetus, killing the mother as well as the child. He had no proof, of course, but he concluded the lie would prevent the integration of half-breeds into the Vampire Nation. You see, he not only hated humans, he feared them. And if half-breeds were allowed to mingle with full vampires, they might be accepted and permitted to play a role in our governance. That, of course, would lead to more mating and even more half-breeds. That was simply untenable.

"And later, when it was discovered that our females had grown barren, that lie shut down the one way we could reproduce and have families. Mating with humans became the answer. The *only* answer. The *forbidden* answer. Acceptance of cross-breeding could have opened many doors—in-vitro fertilization, gestational carriers, surrogacy, and more. Yet the big lie had led to laws against cross-breeding. It became a dead end. So our lives grew desolate, we stagnated, we stopped evolving, and vampires began self-terminating in woeful numbers. A single lie almost killed our nation."

"You have no proof that it *is* a lie," Hannigan roared. "Our scientists have never explored those issues. What proof have you? It has never been disproved. You are the liar, not . . ." He stopped and slumped into his chair, but not before casting a disbelieving glance at Bengotten.

Holmes slapped his hand on the table, his expression furious. "That lie prevented our research. We were afraid we would be accused of heresy. Meanwhile, we have spent more than a century spinning our wheels, desperately seeking answers." He moaned and buried his head in his hands. "So much time and effort wasted. For what? A lie?"

Donovan's expression became solemn. "Members of the Coalition, I have proof of the lie. Irrefutable proof." He walked to the closed doors and flung them open. Shirley and Marilyn, each carrying a baby, walked in. "May I introduce my son, Alexander Jonathan Trait, and my daughter, Lilabeth Constance Trait. Neither exhibited fangs while in the womb and neither has produced fangs since being born." The babies squirmed and babbled. Donovan grinned at them, a proud father to the core.

Bengotten stood and screamed, "They are an abomination! We cannot allow them to exist. They are evil. They will destroy our society." He began to shake with anger. "Seize those children. They must be disposed of."

March glared at him. He took a deep breath and his eyes turned red with fury. "My son and his wife self-terminated because they did not want to live out their lives without children. And I am not alone. How many parents lost family members because they would never have the joy, the laughter, the hope children bring? None of us has forgotten the pure wonder of a child's birth. Watching them grow, explore, learn, and embrace their world. Dammit, our lives have become empty, we have lost purpose, we have become putrid vessels existing for no other purpose than to exist. When it was all a lie?"

Holmes gestured toward Shirley and Marilyn. "May we see them? Prove the lie."

Donovan reached for Alexander. Jonathan took Lilibeth. Carefully, they removed the children from their blankets and held them up in front of the Coalition. "We have human physicians and scientists who will confirm my claim and disprove the lie."

Alexander screwed up his face and a loud emission of flatulence could be heard. Donovan held his son away from him and laughed. "No fangs, but Ye Gods! The smells emitting from their nappies are otherworldly."

Jonathan cradled Lilabeth as her pouty mouth emitted raspberries. "And this one has a set of lungs on her. Our vampire ears are ill-prepared for the noise an infant can make." He smiled. "My Marilyn was a screamer as well. And she became a judge. Maybe Lilabeth will be as well."

Hannigan stood and walked to Donovan, his arms outstretched. "That doesn't negate the agreement you made with the Coalition. We will take possession of these half-breeds now." He cast an evil smile. "Purely for research purposes, of course." He attempted to snatch Alexander from Donovan. "Guards. Take them prisoner."

Donovan stepped away from Hannigan and quickly handed Alexander to Shirley. Then he whistled. The doors opened again, and his mother led a crowd of nuns into the room. They quickly surrounded Shirley, Marilyn, and Jonathan, effectively shielding the babies.

Mother Superior cocked an eyebrow. "We've already been raped, pillaged, and turned by a gang of rogue vampires. We fear nothing and no one. Do your worst, gentlemen. As God is our witness, no harm will come to these children or their family." She nodded at Roger, who was still filming. "We hacked into your cameraman's feed. We have the ability to share these events with your entire nation. Now, that will be good TV. I imagine every one of you will be hunted. You may not fear God, but I imagine thousands of angry vampires with vats of formaldehyde and sharp axes will change your tune." She cackled. "They say there are no atheists in foxholes. I imagine that also holds true for vampires about to have their brains excised from their bodies."

She motioned to Donovan. "Let's be on our way. I do not wish for my sisters to have their souls sullied by such reprehensible beings."

Hannigan again reached for Donovan. Donovan deftly stepped away and quickly packed his briefcase. He tossed the flash drive to March. "I suggest you interrogate Hannigan and his accessory, Bengotten, then lock them up. All the *scientific* evidence you need is on here. I'll give you one week to clean up your mess. Then I unleash this information and this film of this hearing to the masses. And believe me, then they will come for you, *all* of you." He moved into the circle of nuns and moved with them toward the door.

Suddenly, he stopped and turned. "And check your email, *daily*. I have a few suggestions for getting this nation back on the right track."

Donovan grinned. He had no choice really. The family jet was filled with a covey of merry nuns engaged in a very un-nun-like celebration.

Shirley slid her hand into his and giggled. "I'm almost grateful they're nuns. This has the makings of a full-on bacchanalia. I'm not sure that's something I want the twins exposed to at such an early age."

Donovan laughed. "And my mother and Marilyn are right in the middle of it. Poor Dad appears to be somewhat flummoxed. I don't think he has ever been so outnumbered before."

Shirley kissed her husband on the cheek. "You were pretty amazing today. I can't believe we're still on the run until the Coalition reaches a decision. How could they possibly rule against us?"

"They are the Coalition. Their allegiance is to themselves. My arguments were rational, reasonable, and irrefutable, yet those cantankerous old bastards will pursue every possible avenue to remain coddled in their cocoon of ignorance. They haven't changed in centuries. They find security in sameness." Donovan shook his head. "They must be convinced that change is their only way out of this predicament. If they aren't, they could very well retain Bengotten and Hannigan and instead, continue to persecute us."

Shirley frowned. "That makes no sense."

"Which is why we must keep the pressure on. We cannot give up." He cocked an eyebrow. "After our dear sisters recover from their brush with debauchery and repent, we will return to our social media onslaught. I have never been a fan of tweets and tweeters, but we could never have mobilized the vampire world without social media. I am pretty sure the other members of the Coalition have no clue about the power it holds when swaying public opinion. Ye Gods! No one takes power in the human world without it. This is the perfect Twenty-First Century revolution. No guns, No Army. No death. Only words."

Shirley smiled. "Your specialty."

A nun entered from the back of the plane, carrying an energetic Alexander. "I fear Alexander wants to join in the celebration. His sister is sound asleep. He will not settle. Instead, he has been trying to entertain me with giggles and smiles. I thought it best to remove him from the bassinet before he kicked his sister. Little devil."

Shirley reached for him. "And if he was able, I have no doubt he would be sitting among the revelers, hoisting his own bottle of wine. He most definitely favors his father." She stroked the baby's thick black hair. "In looks and temperament. Donovan has always been the life of the party. There was a time when no woman could refuse his charms."

Donovan chuckled. "Until I met the love of my life and lost interest in all that." He removed his son from Shirley's arms and cooed, "You are going to be a chip off the old block, aren't you, son?" He winked at the baby. "I'll have to teach you all of my tricks."

Shirley rolled her eyes. "Please, he's two months old. Can you wait until he is at least a teenager?"

"Of course, dear. Of course." Donovan patted his son on the head. "We would never break a promise to your mother." He smiled at the nun and turned toward the group of rowdy sisters. "I think Alexander and I shall head over there to rescue my poor father. Thank you, Sister Hortense."

Chapter Fourteen: Revolution

Shirley opened her email and hurriedly clicked through her messages. Although she was technically on her honeymoon in the human world, her colleagues on the bench had begun soliciting her opinion on their cases. She didn't mind. It was a way to stay connected to the real world. Life on this island was idyllic, but she couldn't help but miss Chicago. Michigan Avenue. The Magnificent Mile. Restaurants like Alinea, The Girl and the Goat, and Spiaggia. Even Donovan's favorite sports teams — the Bears, the White Sox, and the Bulls. Their life in that city had been filled with excitement.

Shirley stopped at a message from an unknown sender. This was the court intranet. No one else should have access to this server. She waved at one of the nuns. "Sister Marianna. I have a message from an unknown sender. I'm not sure it's safe to open. What should I do?"

Sister Marianna stepped over and studied the screen. She waved at a young man who was seated among the computer users. "Mauricio. We need a security check on a sender."

Mauricio stood up and gazed at Shirley. "Forward it to hinky dinks at the island dot com. I'll trace it. Could be spam or malware. Who knows these days? Do not open it."

Shirley complied. She shut down her laptop and to no one in particular muttered, "Time to feed the monsters." She walked to the exit.

"Miss Shirley." Mauricio waved at her. "You need to see this."

Shirley backtracked to his station. "What is it?"

"It's a letter. From something called the Coalition."

Sister Marianna tapped his arm. "Send your scrubbed version to Miss Shirley and then wipe it from your computer."

Mauricio nodded. "Done."

Shirley pulled out her phone and frantically texted. "Donovan and the others need to see this."

Within minutes, Donovan, Jonathan, Gwendolyn, and Marilyn ran into the room. "What is it?" Donovan gazed at Shirley.

Shirley gestured to her laptop. "A letter from the Coalition."

"Ye Gods, what does it say?"

Shirley peered at the screen. "Dear Lord. and Mrs. Trait— After an extensive interview with Lord Hannigan and Lord Bengotten, and their admissions of guilt, they have been suspended from their duties on the Coalition for a period of one year."

Marilyn gasped. "Those bastards should be exiled, even exterminated. A year is nothing to a vampire. That is barely a slap on the wrist."

Shirley held up a hand. She continued to read, "However, this decision has not been shared with the Vampire Nation and shall remain confidential. Disclosure of said decision and the reasons behind it is prohibited under Coalition decree and carries the force of law."

Donovan snorted. "Idiots. We signed nothing. We agreed to nothing. They think they can pin us to the wall now?"

Shirley gazed at her husband and shook her head. She continued, "Please be advised that all pending charges against you remain. We believe firmly in your guilt and your intention to defy this Coalition. Your utter disrespect for this governing body and our laws is unacceptable. It reveals a lack of civility and adherence to moral code."

Marilyn gasped. "They are accusing us of being immoral?

They are the ones who lied to our nation to engender hate and fear. This is unbelievable."

Shirley sighed. She loved her family, really she did. But they were all strong, opinionated people. She again held up her hand to hopefully stop further rants. "Until your children are surrendered to the proper authorities, the warrant for your arrest and incarceration remains in full force, with the additional charges of sedition stated below. In addition, Lord Jonathan Trait, his wife, Gwendolyn, and daughter, Marilyn, are also charged with sedition, punishable by exile or death.

"At this time, we respectfully request that all parties peacefully surrender to appear before the Coalition for further prosecution and sentencing."

The room went silent. All eyes were focused on Shirley, as if they were looking to her for some direction, some leadership. How had it come to this? One moment she'd been a human, dispensing wisdom from the bench in Chicago. The next she'd been flushed by an IV to remove her human traits and become a creature of the night. All for love. *Only* for love. Yes, this was about love. For her fellow vampires, who had been deprived of the opportunity to create families, give their lives greater meaning. For her fellow half-breeds, who had been turned but not fully accepted into the vampire world, suffering at the hands of a repressive government. And for her new family—her babies, her husband, her sister, mother, and father-in-law. Vampires may not experience love as humans do, but they did reveal affection. They honored tradition. They understood the need to bond.

Now the Coalition had laid down the gauntlet. Shirley slammed her laptop shut. Her eyes narrowed and she gazed at those around her.

"What the bloody, hell," Donovan muttered. "Are they deaf and dumb? Did my words not penetrate their feeble minds?"

Marilyn snarled. "Clearly, they have no respect for any opinion other than their own. And I have no doubt, it was not your words they ignored. They heard you, loud and clear. But you are missing one vital fact. Their lie did not impact men, only women. They had no stake in the outcome, so they care nothing about the impact. It was designed to not only prevent mating with humans and producing half-breeds but also to keep female vamps in their place. As long as we cannot reproduce or raise children, we had no influence. No power."

Jonathan nodded. "That is the only answer that makes sense. The old fools have no idea what we can unleash."

The only proper solution became certain. Shirley pulled out her cell phone and pushed a single button.

Donovan stared at her with horror. "Shirley, what have you done?"

Shirley shook her head. "What we should have done the moment we arrived home. I posted the video of the hearing, the exposure of the great lie, on all vampire social media. The Coalition deserves nothing less. The Vampire Nation will learn the truth and rise up. They will take their nation back."

"But . . ." Donovan swept a hand through his thick hair. "Shirley, you have just declared war. On the Vampire Coalition."

Gwendolyn stepped forward, her eyes filled with pride. She grabbed Shirley's hand and the hand of her daughter. Her smile was luminous. She thrust their hands skyward and proclaimed, "It is about damn time.

"Give us liberty or give us death."

ABOUT THE AUTHOR

Award-winning author Seelie Kay writes about lawyers in love, sometimes with a dash of kink.

Writing under a nom de plume, the former lawyer and journalist draws her stories from more than 30 years in the legal world. Seelie's wicked pen has resulted in twenty works of fiction, including the *Kinky Briefs* series, *The Feisty Lawyers* series, the *Royals Gone Rogue* series, and the *Donovan Trait* series. Other books include *The Garage Dweller, A Touchdown to Remember, The President's Wife, The President's Daughter, Seizing Hope, The White House Wedding, The Last Christmas*, and the romance anthology, *Pieces of Us*.

When not spinning romantic tales, Seelie ghostwrites nonfiction for lawyers and medical professionals. Currently, she resides in a bucolic exurb outside Milwaukee, WI, where she enjoys opera, the Green Bay Packers, gourmet cooking, organic gardening, and an occasional bottle of red wine.

Seelie is an MS warrior and ruthlessly battles the disease on a daily basis. Her message to those diagnosed with this chronic disease: Never give up. You define MS, it does not define you!

Seelie can be found at
www.seeliekay.com,www.seeliekay.blogspot.com,
https://www.instagram.com/seeliekay51,
or on Twitter or Facebook.
To subscribe to her newsletter, please visit
https://rb.gy/w69pim.